Cossmass Infinities

Issue 9

Cossmass Infinities

Issue 9

July 2022

Magazine of Science Fiction and Fantasy Stories

Edited by Paul Campbell

https://www.cossmass.com/

https://www.cossmass.com/

Cossmass Infinities Issue 9 ©2022 by Paul Campbell

ISBN 9798835860258

Cover Art by Grandfailure

Title Font "Snowslider" designed by Samy Halim

A Tomorrow With You In It ©2022 by Matt Tighe
Love Letters ©2022 by Kit Harding
One More Fairy Tale ©2022 by Carol Scheina
A Monster in Miami ©2022 by Daniel Delgado
Home Bound ©2022 by Melanie Bell
Bleed A Little While ©2022 by Michael James
Stasis ©2022 by Lucy Zhang
Sing The End ©2022 by Claire McNerney
Adjectives of Annihilation ©2022 by B. Morris Allen
In the Grip of Yesterday ©2022 by P.A. Cornell
Victorian Resistance & the Lords Insectile ©2022 by M. Legree
Seraph in Ruins ©2022 by Mere Rain
The Long Way Home ©2022 by Tina S. Zhu
Love Like Chocolate ©2022 by Risa Wolf

Contents

Editorial

Welcome the the ninth issue of *Cossmass Infinities*. And sadly the last regular issue.

I want to thank you for reading *Cossmass Infinities*. Your support is vitally important to short fiction magazines like ours.

Unfortunately, *Cossmass Infinities* in its current format can't continue. *I* can't continue it in its current format.

Cossmass Infinities has not found the audience that I had hoped it would. I admit I was naive when I started and leapt in with both feet. Thankfully I haven't spent money I couldn't afford. So far—which is why now is when we have to change.

This is the last of the regular issues. I will continue to publish new stories to the website, and the authors for these stories will continue to be paid at the current SFWA pro-rate. These will be collected into an annual issue, together with a few bonus stories.

In 2021 we had 54 direct subscriptions via PayPal and 22 Patreon members. For the individual issues, (4, 5, and 6), we sold 59, 63, and 41 issues respectively. That amounted to $646.66 (before fees — $518 after) from patrons and

$411.56 ($379.84 after fees) from direct subscribers and $650.37 (before fees) individual issues. (I don't have the split for paperbacks, so I've counted them at the same rate as the ebook to get a rough figure.) Even before fees this only came to $1708.59. The stories for the three issues, plus the bonus stories in The First Year cost $10,057.

I couldn't sustain that.

The Second Year collection will be published on December 1st, and the Third Year collection will be published on July 1st, 2023.

Now, more than ever, I need you to consider helping us to continue by supporting us through Patreon: https://patreon.com/cossmass/

Given time and a growing number of supporters in the new format, I may be able to return to publishing regular issues.

I want to thank you all for your support, for however long it has been.

Our stories this issue begin with *A Tomorrow With You In It* by Matt Tighe. A woman can reverse a death, but she must risk sacrificing something precious from her own future. Kit Harding bring us *Love Letters*. Letters from a runaway girlfriend to her would-be fiance, where she contemplates the ways mental illness can strain relationships, while she wanders the solar system. *One More Fairy Tale* by Carol Scheina. A mother struggles to remain connected to her daughter after her daughter receives genetic modification resulting in extreme sound sensitivity. Daniel Delgado tells of *A Monster in Miami*. A noir fantasy about a Quechua bruja who will do whatever it takes to stop a supernatural killer preying on Indigenous immigrants. *Home Bound* by Melanie Bell. A woman inherits a family home in England...but it comes with a catch. (Set during the Covid Lockdown). Michael James invites us to *Bleed A Little While*. Memory was broken even before the Bleed. *Stasis* by Lucy Zhang. A school of students are stranded in a pocket dimension and try to find a way back home.

In Claire McNerney's *Sing The End* the apocalypse comes in the form of a song, and a singer learns how to build a new life. *Adjectives of Annihilation* by B. Morris Allen. The adults risked everything to leave Earth and find a new home, but now their children want to return. P.A. Cornell makes yet another welcome return with *In the Grip of Yesterday*. An addict experiences the effects of a drug called 'Nostalgia'. *Victorian Resistance & the Lords Insectile* by M. Legree. A doctor devises a horrific bio-weapon to be used against insect invaders. Mere Rain tells of *Seraph in Ruins*. In a war-ruined California, a genetically-engineered soldier finds some new and better reasons to fight. *The Long Way Home* by Tina S. Zhu. Sofia writes love letters across time as she tries to answer her fathers's final question. Risa Wolf sends us off with *Love Like Chocolate*. When Kari discovers she's killing the woman she loves, she quests through her memories to figure out how to save her.

And that is Issue 9. Remember to check our website for more free new stories every month, and look out for The Second Year and The Third Year.

— Paul Campbell *Dundee, Scotland, June 2022*

A Tomorrow With You In It

Matt Tighe

It is dark when they come, banging on the door so loudly that I know they are bringing death with them. I hurry to answer it. I can see you stir in the sleeping alcove, little more than a hump under the blankets, but you are tired out from a day of laughing and climbing and tugging on my skirt, and you do not wake.

The night sounds of the city flow in as I open the door. Hawkers from the late market call and plead over the rise and fall of revellers from a nearby tavern. There is a distant crashing, and then a scream followed by hoarse laughter. Sounds of life, and choice, and chance.

Two men stand on my threshold. One, Iyaan, I know from the market, where he sells the sugared plums you are so greedy for. He has dark hair shot through with grey, and stubble that is more salt than pepper. City life has left its mark on him, but he has kind eyes and an engaging grin. Now, he is serious and pale.

The other is younger. Little more than a man, but he looks as a child with the fear writ large on his face. His eyes are wide, the whites showing all around, and he has been crying. No, he is crying. I start to close the door.

"Please," he says. "Please." He holds out the limp form in his arms, and I curse inwardly. The little girl looks like she is asleep, but she is not. I know that by the way she lays, boneless and still like a broken bird.

I told myself I would not, not again, but she seems so like you. She has the same soft curls, and there is something to the slight upturn of her nose. I am sure it crinkles when she cries. When she cried. Before I can stop myself I reach out. Her skin is soft and cool and her face is calm, but I can see small scarlet droplets in her long eyelashes, and in those dark curls. I feel the tomorrows rent and torn. Here, a flash of dancing in red shoes, giggling with delight. Here, a possible journey, the taste of dust and adventure on parched lips. And here, the bitterness of a first broken heart. The possibilities flail, greying and growing sluggish even as I sense them. My gaze is drawn to you, and then back to this broken creature.

"What happened?" I ask softly.

"She—" the younger man hitches his breath, fights the tears, and then tries again. "She fell. Down the steps. Our home, it is on the west wall."

Simple enough. Such a mundane accident is common enough, too, if you live in one of the city wall slums, rickety buildings that sit atop one another like chipped and uneven stones. The city is full of danger. This you will learn.

"She is dead," I say. I hear the flatness of my own voice, and I hate it. But some things need to be said, before what comes next.

"What would you have of me?"

Both men look uncomfortable in their own ways, and I suppress a sigh. You will find that most people cannot give voice to the impossible, no matter how much they want it.

————

It has been long, and longer, since I have been asked to do this. There was a time when such as I, such as we, were more common, but we are not built to last. Chance and choice take us early if we persist. I do not want to do it—I hope you believe that. But she is so like you. And she would have had red shoes, or an adventure, or heartache. Or so many other tomorrows.

"Put her on the rug," I say. You have not wakened, and I doubt you will. You sleep the deepest of sleeps, as I did as a child before you. Time enough for sleeplessness when you are older, when you give away the tomorrows that you have. Oh, my love, please have more care than I.

The younger man lays the girl down in the middle of our small living space, and I motion for him to step back. What I am to do is both simple and the hardest thing. I glance to you again, but not to check your sleep. I should not do this thing, should not risk what I risk, but she has those curls, and had those tomorrows. How can I turn away those that have come? Am I so selfish as to risk nothing?

"You must promise," I say, turning to hold my visitors with my eyes.

"Anything!" the young man sobs, and Iyaan nods quickly.

"Two things," I continue, without acknowledging their hastiness. "First, you must not tell others." Here, I fix Iyaan with a cold eye and he has the grace to blush. It makes him more than handsome. I can see the remnants of the child he was, before the city marked him with its weight. My heart twists a little.

"Second," I continue. "If something happens to me, tomorrow or the next day or maybe months from now, you must promise to care for mine, if no one else makes a claim you think is just." It has been long since I have done this thing, and extracted such a promise. I do not know if my last visitors would still consider themselves bound, as belief in strange things dwindles so with time. But Iyaan has those kind eyes, and his friend cries so for his lost daughter. They are both good things, so I ask.

There is a moment of silence as they digest my words. Iyaan's eyes widen, and he makes as if to speak. I raise one hand to stop him. I look at the younger man, the girl's father, and I see what I need there on his face. Hope, and pain, and perhaps, the small beginnings of understanding.

I kneel by the girl. I do not search for her injuries. They are not important. I do not know where this gift, or this curse, or both, comes from. I know it was in my mother, and I feel it in your small, chubby hands as they grasp mine. It is much the same as I feel from others, twisting threads of chance, but in yours, I feel this curse, this skill, this risk, winding its way through your days.

In the girl, the threads are torn and fading. I see again the red shoes, taste the dust and thirst, feel the heartache. And more besides, but now they are all like whispers, sun-faded paintings, echoes. I turn to regard the men. Their pathways are strong, bright and silver. The girl's father has but a handful left to him, even at his young age. In one, he is destitute, bereft, a failure. In several others, he dies early, but not completely unhappy. There are a few wavering, silvery threads of hope still there, hovering about him, stretching up and away to a future that may grow from a miracle.

Iyaan is different. His pathways are few, and gleam with solid chances of becoming. I am a little surprised to see one silvery line flash with an image of me, bright and twisting with emotion. With an effort, I put my desire to trace it, to see what I can see, aside. You must do the same, when fate tempts you. You will never see enough, and the taste of those bright threads of chance are so very bitter.

I look back to the girl. I know what she would have had, if I had seen her earlier. Silvery threads of possible futures spilling out of her, splitting, merging, twisting and branching, choices made and ignored, her many lives flickering as possibilities. Now, there are just those fading threads, the last flickers of a fire that has burnt to embers.

I reach up to my own threads. There are not that many of them, and I do not see them as clearly as I see others. I let my fingers brush one, then another. There is an art to what I do, to what you may feel compelled to do. You need one that will take root, but you must select so very carefully. The first I touch has the smell of flatbread and long, warm summer days, the ache of old bones. It fills me with both satisfaction and tiredness. It is not of interest to a young girl on the edge of life. The second is nothing but tears and hollowness, and I push it away from me. The third—there is a flash of laughter and childish spirits. I draw in a sharp breath as I see you, smiling and spinning, watching your dress twirl in the late afternoon sun. You are older, but not much, and I feel an ache inside as I close my hand around the thread. It will work.

I pluck the thread even as my eyes well with tears. I have not changed the chance you will spin and smile—I cannot do that. But if that future firms and grows, I will not see it.

I give the thread to the girl. She is young, and there was at least a possibility that she would one day dance and giggle in red shoes. It is enough. The thread catches and holds and shimmers. It will grow and split and spread, choices wending their way back into her tomorrows. The rootstock is strong and well-matched.

The girl breathes deeply and her father cries out. I slump back on my haunches and wave at them to leave me be. I am not tired, but I ache inside. The image of you spinning and smiling is fading, and I feel...I don't know. Less. Ashamed. I should be able to say no. I cannot say no. I do not understand myself, and yet I hope one day you will.

Iyaan hustles the man and his daughter away, shushing them both as they cry, him in relief, her in confusion. He whispers to me he shall return to see me later, but I do not want to look for that thread that may run from him to me. It was the future, and it was only a chance anyway.

———

My tea cools in my hand as I sit by the window, listening to the city, listening to the choices being made, the futures winnowed from silvery chance. I order my thoughts as best I can, but it is hard. Soon, I will write the story of tonight, and hope you will one day hear it from my lips, rather than read it on old, dry parchment.

What I do is what I must, but I don't know if I can keep on, or if I should. I close my eyes and see a young girl, dancing in red shoes. I try to see you, spinning in the afternoon sun, and I cannot. It is nothing but the memory of a day I will never see. The memory of a tomorrow with you in it.

© 2022 Matt Tighe

Fantasy - 1880 words

About the Author

Matt Tighe lives in south eastern Australia with his amazingly patient wife, not so patient children, and the unlikely duo of Sherlock the dog and Moriarty the cat. He is an academic in his other life. His work has appeared in *Nature Futures*, *The NoSleep Podcast*, and *Spawn: Weird Horror Tales about Pregnancy, Birth and Babies* from IFWG Australia as well as other places. He enjoys running and posting photos of the same run many, many times on social media. You can find such on twitter **@MKTighewrites** and other info at https://matttighe.weebly.com/ (including a cool picture his son drew of his father's brain).

Love Letters

Kit Harding

Dear Sam,

I'm sorry. I know this isn't what you wanted. I just wanted to reassure you that I'm still alive since I know you probably didn't believe Grant when he told you I wasn't planning my own death.

I suppose you want an explanation, but I don't have a good one to offer. I ran away. I admit that. I came to Mars for you, because I love you, but it's so stifling there. Everything is all chrome and glass, and no one can leave the dome or go outside. There's no weather, there's no sun, there's no sky. It all just seems so soulless and mechanical. I know you like it, but you were born there. I was born on Earth, and for all that we've ruined the climate, it's still home—and if everyone who can dream leaves for the colonies, we'll have no one left to repair the damage.

I've been avoiding thoughts of the future since I met you. Long distance relationships are always rough, and interplanetary ones are hell on the people involved. Deep down, I always knew something would have to break. Either one of us would have to move, or we'd have to end things. I wasn't expecting you to propose—and really, Sam, proposing without warning when we live on different planets? Just assuming that of course I would move to Mars? How exactly were you *expecting* that to go?

Don't answer that; I can guess exactly how you expected that to go. Just so you know, I'm rolling my eyes right now.

I need to be alone for a while, to get my head clear. I won't be checking email or answering my phone. I'm going to walk the worlds for a bit; see if being somewhere with no history helps. If you want to communicate, I'll make sure the post office knows where I am, so letters can find me. (If you're about to complain about how archaic and expensive sending a letter is, I'm aware. That's the idea. It forces you to think about what you're saying.)

Of course, if you want to wash your hands of me, I understand. Even if I told Grant I was leaving, from your perspective, I did just vanish for a week with no word. If you want to write, I'll be here.

Amelia

————

Dear Sam,

I appreciate your willingness to abide by my terms. No, I don't have a plan. Isn't that what finding yourself is? If you walk long enough, you figure out what you want. At least, I hope to.

It may amuse you to know that my status as an agony aunt remains undiminished even among strangers. I was sitting in a café with a spectacular view of the rings when a girl came up, sat down at my table, and just started pouring out her tale. She'd moved out to Titan to look after her mother, and now her mother had passed and she was still out on Titan where she had no desire to be, with no idea where to go or what to do. She didn't have any money to go elsewhere, and she didn't have any life here—but when I asked she also said she didn't really have any idea where she did want to be, or anyone waiting for her on any other planets. She started on Earth but there was nothing strong drawing her back to it; her world drifted away from her as though she'd never been there when she left. No strong roots, just a tumbleweed among the stars.

I'll own that I'm a little skeptical that anyone who can sit down in a café and start randomly telling this sort of tale to a complete stranger is having difficulty socializing. (Or perhaps that's the problem, lack of boundaries.) Do I exude a field or something? 'Will listen and offer gentle-but-sage advice drawn from wide reading and horrible life experiences?' Everyone in your studio was pouring out their hearts after I'd been there all of a day. I don't mind it, exactly, but all that emotion gets overwhelming—though it is much easier to deal with other people's problems. I'm as lost as she is in some ways, but I can give her suggestions that are actually helpful. Look through the hobby sites on my StarPad, show her where she can find some groups that do things she's always had a vague interest in, so she can try it out. Talk about how you have to be patient with friendships. Well, that one I know firsthand, for sure. How long did you and I circle each other at game conventions before we admitted it wasn't a parasocial relationship?

Honestly, it's hard for me to imagine. Not the lack of close ties—I certainly didn't have people who'd miss me when I was younger—but the lack of feeling rooted. Earth is my core. Boston is the center of the solar system. There is no skyline more beautiful than Boston at night, as viewed from the harbor. The smell of the salt, and sometimes the stench of what the gulls leave behind. To stand on a beach as the ocean lashes it and the wind tears at your clothing, with the sun or storm or stars above you. Maybe it's different if you're born to the stars, but I'm not one of the galaxy's children.

Amelia

———

Dear Sam,

Being born on Earth doesn't count if you didn't spend any time actually living there. You were on Mars before you were a year old. It's where you grow up that matters. You were shaped by the hiss of the recycled air and the restrictions of the dome and the constant safety drills. I've been having safety drills every time I take passage on a new ship or arrive at a new planet, in addition to the regular ones if I stay in one place too long. There was enough distance between them on Mars that I could almost let it slip to the back of my mind that the air was dependent on mechanics that could easily fail, but when I'm traveling, drills are so frequent, it's impossible to forget.

I know you'd say a planet is just as fragile, given what we did to the climate of ours. But it took a lot of people many generations to do that. It's not the work of a moment—a single leak, a single mistake, a single component failure.

Excepting that ever-present worry, Mercury station isn't bad. There's not a lot going on here—they don't get a lot of visitors—but it does have beautiful views. Most of the station is science labs and most of the people here are scientists, but there's also an observation deck, so I've been painting sunscapes. I really think this could be an artists' haven if people looked at the way space stations work more rationally. Once you've accepted that all that's standing between you and death is a bit of metal, you're not going to get more dead just because that metal is practically on top of the sun. Yes, I don't like that entire sensation, but there are plenty of artists who don't mind space travel in general but don't want to come to Mercury station because it's so close to the sun. The whole thing is silly.

The upside is everyone here is very friendly! I get the impression they're bored. Do science all day, talk about science all night, never have the chance to see new people. I'm an exciting change of pace! (You can stop laughing now.) I might stay a while; I'm enjoying the company. I spent a couple of *enjoyable* nights with one of the scientists, for example. (It's just fun. I know that, they know that, and whatever our current relationship state you and I were never exclusive. So don't start lecturing me about making impulsive decisions in my fragile state.)

Grant wrote me a letter too. He says you haven't been speaking to him except for when you need to for the show.

Do I have to tell you how ridiculous you're being? Or how patronizing that attitude is? I *made my own choices.* He just listened to me talk everything out and kept my confidences private. For the record, he didn't think this was a good idea—but he also respects my freedom of choice.

Why did I talk to him and not you? You're not objective. You want me to be on Mars. You *proposed,* Sam. That's about as involved as it gets. You want to know what Grant told me? That if I was that torn up about you proposing, I should spend some time trying to understand why. That it *was* a choice, that I didn't have to do what everyone expected of me. That if I needed to get away, there were less drastic ways to do that than death.

He didn't *make* me have doubts. I had the doubts on my own. He just helped me find a way to think about them.

Amelia

————

Dear Sam,

I never realized how big Jupiter's spot was until I was looking at it directly. It's enormous, and very red. Pictures don't do it justice. I had a lot of trouble getting it into a canvas, too, though I have been trying. No painting ever matches the images I have in my head. Nothing ever does, really. I wonder if that's why we're all so driven to create—I make these paintings, you write your soap opera, Grant directs it... We spend our lives trying to live up to the images we have in our heads. Every time I paint something, it's closer, but it never gets there. Who am I? Who are you? How can I share what can't be shared, that sense of perception?

I'm apparently feeling philosophical today. Wandering does that to you. The worlds pass by one after another. You stay on them for a few days or weeks, you converse but form no relationships; the press of humanity flows around you but does not touch you. We have claimed our solar system, but the stars are still out there. I'm sitting in a café on a shopping concourse in a station that would have been the product of dreamers a century ago. But when I'm on Earth, looking up at the sky from there...we've never touched another star. There's so much more to the solar system than what we see. There's more wonder looking up at it from down there.

I know, I know, you get lost when I get all philosophical like this. You prefer the concrete realities of the world around us. I still haven't found what I'm looking for. I thought this would be easier. I thought it would be a few weeks of wandering and I'd know all the answers. All I'm finding is distance, and all that's left is being alone with my thoughts. I've always tried not to be alone with my thoughts because that's when I start wanting to die. I think shutting it out for so long may have been a mistake because there are times when I'm standing on a concourse or in a ship or alone in a hostel room and it just *hits* me, and then I want to punch a wall or slice my skin off. You don't have those moments, the times where the memory becomes so overpowering it's all you can see. I thought if I kept moving my emotions wouldn't catch up to me, but that's not how it works. It's not *finite*.

Amelia

———

Dear Sam,

I've *been* in treatment. I have brain meds, remember? I'm visiting space stations with regular trade routes and functional pharmaceutical manufacturing; getting my prescriptions filled isn't hard. And once I'm done traveling I'll have therapy again. I've never been averse to treatment. I'm averse to having my choices taken away.

But there are limits even to the most successful of treatments. I'm making long trips on small spaceships with few distractions. Sometimes it gets to me, and I deal with it when it does. Sometimes I have awful moments. That's never going to stop.

I'm out here to do art. I'm out here to have adventures. Most of all I'm out here to get away. There's no pressure, going from planet to planet. No one knows who I am. No one has any expectations. It's freeing. And I have common sense, which is more than I can say for the teenagers on this station. One of them took one of the little skimmers way deeper into the asteroid belt than it was meant for. He was going to stay out there for months 'exploring', except skimmers can't actually handle months, and he'd disabled all the search beacons so no one could find him and drag him home. Search and Rescue mobilized once they realized a skimmer was missing, but there's only so fast they can go without a beacon or an accurate flight plan.

I was by the main airlock when they brought his body back. It's in a capsule, so I didn't actually *see* the body, but...you know what's in there, when you see one of those capsules. He's not *from* here—kids who grow up stationside know better than to pull stunts like that—so there wasn't any weeping family at the airlock, but there's going to be, somewhere else.

There are some things I can't paint, you know?

Amelia

————

Dear Sam,

Oddly enough, I am aware you were concerned I was dead. I acknowledged that in my first letter to you, remember? You chose not to wash your hands of me. Nor did I come out here looking for death; if I had I wouldn't still be writing to you. And you're still listed as my emergency contact. If I was found dead, notification would get to you much faster than the letters do.

You say my illness worries you. It worries me, too, but in different ways. Death isn't the only thing, or even the worst thing, I'm afraid of. What's the point in being alive if you wrap me in cotton wool for my own safety?

They make rings that read your pulse point and transmit it to the other ring so you can always feel your lover's heartbeat against your hand. They're shockingly expensive because of how reliable they are. Someone on Mercury station can feel the heartbeat even if their partner's on Pluto with only a minute or so of delay. Your heartbeat can break the speed of light so that you always know. No matter where you are, you know your lover is alive.

If I wore one of those, would it set you at ease? If you could wear a matching one, and always know I'm still alive, would that make this easier to live with?

Because I don't think it would. You aren't afraid that I'm dead *now*; you're afraid I will become so in some nebulous future. But there are a thousand possible causes for that. Is dying by my own hand so much worse than dying if an airlock fails, or a skimmer crashes? Is it so much more frightening if I die like that? I was *sixteen* the first time I seriously considered suicide. This isn't going to just go away, no matter how much you'd like it to.

Amelia

————

Dear Sam,

I visited the Last Horizon landing site today. It's so small for something so significant. Pluto hadn't been a planet for a century when they launched it. There were hundreds of objects in the Kuiper Belt. But they came out here anyway. They launched from Mars—from the Sagan Memorial Observatory—in a time when it wasn't an easy trip. They took months to get here. And for what? To say they'd sent a manned mission to Pluto? There's such history here. I would have liked to visit the Observatory while I was on Mars. I may not have a starfarer's spirit—not properly—but I'm still a dreamer. I still see the poetry.

They came out here just so they could say they could. Almost all space travel has been like that. Hell, you go back far enough...people went to the South Pole just to say they could. I admire that strength of character. It takes a lot of confidence and nerve to stare death in the face and keep going forward.

I don't think I could do it. I know, that seems weird to you given my history, but there's a difference between taking your own life and something else taking it for you. The sense of control, maybe. It always seems to come back to control. Maybe that's what it is—if I uproot my life to join you on Mars, then I'm losing that control. I can paint anywhere, yes, but the place where I have the connections to survive, to support myself...that's all on Earth. If I go to Mars I lose that, and what's left? What's left when you take away everything I am?

That's what broke, that night. I didn't want to look at it, because once it was in the open our breakup was inevitable. I'm not willing to uproot my life for you. I belong to Earth. To an atmosphere that isn't trying to kill me and flowers that grow naturally and the slow process of healing the ecological damage. But you can't uproot your life for me either. You have friends and a wonderfully creative job and theater and community. No matter how much I want to be with you, and I do love you, the practicalities are always going to be between us. It was an impossible choice, and I couldn't see a way forward.

Yes, leaving was an impulse. But things are simpler out here. I'm managing on my own. My life isn't collapsing without you in it. I'm here. I'm *fine.*

I appreciate the fact that you've been writing, that you gave me the chance to have this gentler goodbye than it otherwise would have been, to let this fade through slow realization instead of abrupt and painful collapse. So yes, this is where I leave you. Letters will still find me. Your letters will always find me. But they'll be different letters. Bittersweet letters of friendship, not all-consuming ones of passion. I'm going home now, to stay. I'm sure I'll see you a few days after you get this letter because you'll want to change my mind, but I'm certain of my decision.

I'm sorry it couldn't have been different. Under other circumstances, I would have been thrilled to marry you. If there was less pulling us apart...but there isn't.

People don't talk enough about circumstances, in relationships. They say 'love conquers all', as though that means something. And it doesn't. Not enough.

Then again, if I'd known that I'd never have pursued you in the first place. And despite everything, I don't regret our relationship.

Ever yours,

Amelia

© 2022 Kit Harding

Science Fiction - 3177 words

About the Author

Kit Harding is a writer and librarian who belongs to the cities and wilds of New England. Her work has also appeared in the Zombies Need Brains anthology *Derelict* and in *Luna Station Quarterly*. You can find her online at https://writerkit.dreamwidth.org/ and check out her podcast at https://www.mtgnexus.com/.

One More Fairy Tale

Carol Scheina

I was told you were dead, but I knew that wasn't the true story. A mother always knows. I still have one more fairy tale to tell you, my daughter, even if you never hear it from my lips.

Once upon a time, there was a woman who badly wanted a child, the longing pinpricking at her heart until she couldn't ignore it. People with those kinds of longings always make deals, and this time around, that person was me.

The deal was simple: DefenseCorp would give me one of their engineered kids to raise as my own. I worked for DefenseCorp, so it was easy to get permission. No one liked the thought of children being raised in compounds, even if they were bred and born in glass containers. Even if they were to be soldiers when they grew up. Children were still children, so they were all too happy to let me take a child.

A baby girl. You.

In fairy tales, such deals always go wrong. The witch steals the child away to a tower, or some little imp with a funny name tricks everyone. But I didn't consider what could go wrong when I signed the paperwork. I imagined a small hand grasping my finger, toothless baby grins in the morning.

I signed away, and in a blink, you became mine.

Remember those storybooks we used to read together? We'd squish into that saggy old floral chair, a thick tome upon our shared laps, our minds overflowing with imagined worlds. I'd finish a story about trickster spiders, then we'd move on to griffins in the sky. Then I'd tell you a real story—all about the portal being constructed and the work I was doing with DefenseCorp. They didn't just do soldiers, you know; they also funded science. They funded me, to make my theories on multi-world travel a reality.

Once upon a time, the act of slipping between worlds could only be done in stories, but soon, not anymore. We'd snuggle together and wonder if those imagined places in our books could be real, waiting for us somewhere out there.

"Mommy, can we find the fairy tale world out there?" you asked.

I kissed your head. "We'll find it."

"And do battles and have adventures and happily ever after?"

"Absolutely, baby girl." I tilted my head closer, to take in the scent of the cinnamon milk you always drank. To have my lips brush the soft curls on your head.

Ever wonder why people in fairy tales make deals? It's for the moments like that.

I'd have made another one in a heartbeat if I could have stopped time.

But quick as a fairy godmother's wave of the wand, you transformed into an 18-year-old with too-long limbs and a lopsided smile. DefenseCorp came calling.

There's always a catch, you see. You were never really mine.

They advised caretakers not to watch, but I was there, watching behind glass windows as the machines stabbed your eyes and ears, pumping them full of nanobots. Instead of reading fairy tales, your enhanced eyes would scan the horizon for the slightest quiver of enemy movement. Your ears weren't enhanced for bedtime stories but for the sound of footsteps a mile away.

They said I'd be asked to leave if I got emotional, so I hid the tears in the corners of my eyes and fixed a porcelain smile on my face. That's why you never saw them, but they were there.

The nurses moved you to a sensory-safe room to recover, with gray padded walls and near-dark bulbs recessed far into the ceiling. But a nurse failed to shut the door fast enough, and you bolted up, hands over your ears, a scream on your lips: "Please, turn it off!"

Turn what off?

Afterward, the nurse told me it was probably a trolley on another floor. What did it sound like to you? I imagined your eardrum turning into a blackboard, each wheel-squeak a fingernail scrape against your brain, thrumming on nerves, vibrating deep into your mind.

Pain I wanted to suck out of your ears, pain I would've gladly taken instead of you. I didn't tell you that.

I cheered when the doctor gave you extra recovery time at home with me. You were mine again, just for a little longer, even if your ears were covered with mufflers to block out the sound that still ripped at you.

I pulled a cheerful voice out from somewhere deep inside me. "Okay, time to take off the mufflers!" As though we were heading out on a mother-daughter date to the spa.

But this is what the doctor wanted me to do, to help you get used to the enhanced sounds. It would help you, right?

Me sitting in the saggy floral chair, you on the couch, me missing those days when you were small enough to squeeze in beside me and I could hug your fears away. Your shoulders drawn up, your hand moving so deliberately, regret in every motion, you'd gingerly pull off the mufflers.

You were becoming a soldier, too old for fairy tales, so that's why I softly read the Soldier's Handbook.

Your shoulders spasmed. Your fingernails formed red crescents in your palms, on the verge of bleeding.

Did my voice break apart into an octave of needles, each finding a different section of your brain to stab, sharp and deep? I wanted to rip my words to pieces.

I could see my voice never got easier for you, despite all the doctor's reassurances.

You remember the day you asked me to escape?

"Where would we go?" I asked.

"To another world."

"The portal's still being developed. It's too dangerous."

I replay that conversation in my mind a lot. The way your body shut up like a closed book. "It's okay," you whispered.

"I'm sorry, I can't change this." I squeezed your hand.

"I know. I don't blame you. I still love you." Your eyes turned down.

I blamed myself. I wanted to re-write the way this tale was going.

The words between us slowed. What could we say to each other except for words of pain? And then you were gone to do your military service. You were never really mine.

But you really were. I should've told you that.

I didn't know you had volunteered to work on the trans-world portal. My theory, finally made real. Someone had volunteered to be the first to go through. I didn't know it was you.

The next time I heard about you was when a DefenseCorp representative with carefully manicured hair showed up at our home. I sat in the floral chair as he recited the official report in a soothing voice: "You're listed as the point of contact, which is why we are required to inform you that this soldier volunteered to test an experimental device." He fumbled with the explanation, but he was a paper pusher, not a scientist. I kept my face a closed book.

The man continued, "We lost contact with her." The words 'presumed dead' were followed by too many empty phrases about heroism.

People saw a brave soldier when you stepped through the portal and vanished.

But I'd known your story by heart for years; I had a feeling it wasn't yet over. Call it a mother's instinct that you knew what you were doing when you left the world of your birth.

It took some digging through my charts of the other worlds, but I found the place where there's no sound at all. I knew at once that had become your new world.

It still seems like a fairy tale, knowing that there are other worlds nestled in dimensions right next to ours. Like two eggs side by side, and with just the slightest pressure, the shells crack, and a tiny bit can drip into another.

I knew how to crack the barrier.

Into my backpack went the essentials—food, rope, a flashlight, a knife. You don't need all the details of how I snuck past security, how I activated the trans-world portal. Just know that I stepped into another world for you. You're my daughter. Of course I was going to follow you.

My first sight through the portal was emerald leaves, each as thick as a tree, covered with curling brown vines towering toward the sun. For all my studies, I didn't expect the heaviness of the atmosphere pressing on my shoulders. My ears played ringing music to fill the smothered emptiness. Even knowing that the atmosphere wouldn't allow sound, I couldn't help but call your name, and the air jiggled like a pudding, absorbing my voice.

Vines curled toward the vibrations, stretching for my face. When I gasped and jumped back, the tendrils snapped closer, barbed ends prodding the empty space near me. After I closed my mouth to stop any further air quivers, the vines hesitated, then coiled away.

In the leaves above me, I saw the remains of a tentacled creature, like a cross between a cow and a squid. The vines had planted their spines into the beast to drink the sunset-hued liquid inside.

Blood and silence. That's the world you'd chosen.

It struck me that stepping into another world isn't like reading a book. You can't close it and be safe again in your floral chair.

But I found a safe space, a clearing where the browns and greens gave way to fine white sand rolling into dunes. There, a distance away from the penetrating vines, was a military-issue tent and a campfire with something meat-like roasting over it.

There, I saw you.

My heart screamed your name, and you looked up, almost like you were drawn to the vibrations of my love, my joys, my fears, my regret, my hopes, all tightly compressed into the thick air.

As I ran to you, far too sluggish in the shifting sand and thick air, my mind played, once more, the story I want to tell you. The story that's been in my mind all this time. The story you will never hear from my mouth, not in this silent world, but you can read it in my eyes, see in my heart.

When you pull me close into a hug, I brush my lips against your hair, and I can almost smell cinnamon milk in your breath.

I brought two books with me: one is a book of an old language of the hands. We don't need sound to talk. We don't need to hear ever again.

And the second is a blank book, for us to write our own fairy tale.

We can still find that happily ever after. It all begins now, you and me, with a once upon a time.

© 2022 Carol Scheina

Science Fiction - 1808 words

About the Author

Carol Scheina is a deaf speculative fiction author from the Northern Virginia area. Many of her stories were thought up while sitting in local traffic, resulting in tales that have appeared in *Daily Science Fiction*, *Escape Pod*, *The Arcanist*, and other publications. You can find more of her work at https://carolscheina.wordpress.com/.

A Monster in Miami

Daniel Delgado

I really shouldn't be here, I thought as soon as I saw the body.

The dead man had been spread on the marshy ground at the shore of the mangrove swamp, next to the fishermen's canoe. The boat was beached at one of the few breaks in a dense mass of mangrove roots that sprawled explosively into the air before plunging down and vanishing into the green-gray water.

His head had been removed, leaving behind most of the neck, and a wicked slash gaping at the base of his throat. His hands had been chopped off just above the wrists.

The body was shirtless and barefoot. It had a slightly shrunken, dried-out look that I assumed came from its time in the saltwater.

But what do I know? I'm a *bruja*, not a forensic scientist.

"What the hell did you call me for?" I snapped in Spanish, feeling the beginnings of panic. "Why didn't you call the damn cops?"

Just a half-hour ago, I'd been driving home from a sleepless night battling a particularly vicious *duende* that had taken up in a sweet old lady's fig tree. I'd been halfway back to my parents' house when the call came, summoning me urgently to this deserted park at the outskirts of Coral Gables.

Now here I was: blinking sweat and sleep from my eyes; gnats swarming at my face; my flats *splish*ing alarmingly in the spongy ground. My tight jeans and form-hugging, long-sleeve shirt clung damply, chafingly.

The men exchanged a glance, and I immediately felt foolish. Maybe they were just out here fishing without a license, but more than likely at least one of them was undocumented.

"Right," I said. "No police. But why me?"

The fishermen were stocky and short, with classically Indigenous Andean features—bold noses, prominent cheekbones, and skin the color of wet sand. I placed them in their mid to late 40s. They both wore jeans and casual long-sleeve, button-down shirts. In other words, they were typical clients for Ana María Quispe Ruiz, *la Bruja de Miami.*

Honestly, they could have been my uncles. I've got the same Native features, the same compact, though curvier, build.

One of the men—Severino, he'd said his name was—gestured helplessly at the body. "He was killed by a pishtako," he said.

I felt the bottom drop out of my stomach. "How do you know?"

The other man, Arturo, knelt beside the body, visibly braced himself, and rolled it onto its belly. Two large holes had been cut in the lower back, on either side of the spine.

Nauseated, fascinated, I crouched down to stare at the wounds.

"Did they...take out his *kidneys*? But that's...not right at all. Pishtakos take the fat, not the organs."

Severino set me straight with a curt shake of his head. "Now, in the *sierra*, they come sometimes for the kidneys or the corneas. They sell them on the international organ market."

I was fascinated despite myself. The pishtako was an old monster, at least as old as the *Conquista*. The earliest stories my grandparents knew were of Spanish priests who accosted solitary Indians and drained their bodies of fat, which they used to oil their church bells. The newest were of light-skinned Limeños or foreigners, who used the fat for anything from military hardware to global cosmetics.

The college-educated North American in me thought, *How natural for the tale to evolve like this. The original story melds perfectly with modern urban legends.*

But the traditionally educated, Peruvian *bruja* heard herself murmuring, "The kidneys are covered in a layer of fat."

Europeans and their descendants say that blood is the source of life. But in the highlands of the Andes, we know: blood has power, but the *life*…that's in the fat.

My hands moved to the body's bare feet, pushing up the cuffs of the pants. The skin around the ankles was scraped away.

It all fit. It fit *both stories.*

In the stories my grandparents had told me, pishtakos cut off their victims' hands and heads, then hoisted them by the ankles over a fire, to melt the fat and drain it from the body. And it looked like the victim had been killed by a single slash at the throat, the pishtako's classic MO. Hell, for all I knew the absent head was even missing its eyes, to further match the newer version.

If fit. But…

I fixed the men with my most piercing stare. They were twice my age, but they flinched.

"What else?" I said. "This could be any random sicko. It could be a mob killing. *So why did you call me?*"

Severino licked his lips. "People have been disappearing. For a while now, one every few months. All of them are recent immigrants, *cholos*."

He used the word in the Andean sense, not the Mexican one. He meant Indians or at least people who 'looked like' Indians.

People like us.

"But you know, people disappear sometimes. It could have been anything," Severino said. "Then we saw this…" He gestured helplessly.

I shook my head. "But a pishtako is just a human being," I said. "A monster, yes, but not a magical one. What do you expect me to do about this?"

They just stared at me. And I thought, if I were them, what would I do?

I would go to someone I could trust, of course.

So what if I didn't want to be that person? So what if I was twenty-three and barely out of my apprenticeship? So what if I'd never faced anything worse than a *duende* or a restless spirit?

They had come to me.

I indulged myself in one last sigh, then I nodded and got to work.

————

The first thing I did was tie my long, dark hair up and out of my face. Then I swept the area for anything important that the fisherman might have missed. Nothing new turned up, other than the blood-stained jute sack the men had found the body in. I gingerly set the sack alongside the corpse.

Out came my *bolsa*, or my 'working bag', as I like to call it. It's a small, waterproof backpack-purse with about a dozen pockets that I keep stocked with the charms, herbal medicines, and sacred plants I'm most likely to need on the fly. I hesitated for a moment, then pulled out a small ziplock bag filled with coca leaves. I hated to use them, as they're damn hard to come by in this country. But they're the most powerful divinatory herb I know, and this didn't seem like the time to hold back.

I said a brief prayer to Mama Coca, in Spanish as my grandmother had taught me, wishing as always that I knew the words in Quechua. "Guide me," I prayed, "and help me to protect your people." A soothing presence settled around my shoulders, and I felt some of my tension bleed away.

With careful concentration, I passed the leaves from the top of the body to the base of the feet, then turned and cast them onto an open patch of ground.

I'd never worked with a dead body before, so I was pretty much making this up as I went along. The ritual I was performing, in fact, was actually a diagnostic for a sick, but living, person. I doubted that anything would come of it.

The coca leaves hit the ground, broken and scattered, each piece at least an inch from its nearest neighbor. I whistled softly. All the leaves had been whole when I started—I'd made sure of it.

The body was dead, yes, but the leaves suggested something worse than a severed head.

If the pishtako is a monster from a horror story, then it's a story laced with irony. Because what does the monster do with the sacred, life-giving fat that it's willing to commit murder to possess?

Nothing, not really. Certainly nothing that makes use of the potent spiritual power that fat holds. At the end of the day, the pishtako is a vulgar foreigner, blind to spiritual truth and in thrall to hollow gods. He steals sacred life force only to profane it with crass materialism.

But Mama Coca was telling me that this body's spiritual self had been savaged.

I pulled out a bag of *mapacho*, a more powerful cousin to the tobacco you can buy at the store. After a prayer to Mama Mapacho, I poured some of the dried leaves into a ceramic bowl and used a lighter to get them smoking.

I raised the bowl before the body, breathed deeply, then puffed out sharply. Then I waved the bowl back and forth over the body to create a thick cloud. I could feel my vision sharpening, showing me a glimmer of the spiritual world.

I stepped back, horrified. A spiritual miasma, a pulsing darkness, hung over the corpse. Tendrils of sickness oozed from the main mass, swaying as if seeking a victim to grab. I looked down. I could see the sickness clinging to my clothing. It was worse around Severino and Arturo; it hung heavy around their heads and shoulders, and had already started to seep into their eyes, noses, and mouths.

I took fast, deep breaths, fighting back panic. I gestured the men over and blew the smoke over their faces, then fanned it back over my own body. My healer's sight was fading, but I could already see the sickness starting to retreat.

I waved away their worried questions and frowned at the body, thinking. I couldn't back out of this, not now. And that meant I needed some way to track the monster.

Normally, I would clip a few hairs from the victim and use that to anchor a spell. Obviously, that wasn't an option.

And with spiritual contagion hanging so dense over the body, I certainly wasn't going anywhere near the blood.

A moment's queasy consideration, and a pair of nail clippers came out of my *bolsa*. I said a prayer for the unknown *cholo*'s soul.

Or whatever was left of it.

Then I bent to clip the nails from his bare feet.

————

I promised Severino and Arturo—somewhat disingenuously—that I had the matter under control. I told them to head directly home and wait for me to call them to set up appointments for a proper healing ritual, a *despacho*. I warned them not to do anything that would expose them to spiritual contamination. They seemed properly intimidated.

I'm ashamed to admit it, but we put the body back in the bag and tossed it in the swamp for the crocodiles. I did say a prayer first and promised to offer coca leaves and corn with the toenails when I was done with them. I tried to tell myself that a water burial was something that our Amazon-dwelling ancestors might have done. But the truth is that there was simply no way for us to get out of that park carrying a decapitated body in a bloody sack. And where would we have even buried it?

I tried not to think about how I'd *just said* the fishermen should avoid spiritual contamination. I also tried not to think about who would do a *despacho* for me if the mapacho hadn't done the trick.

When I got back to my car, the first thing I did was drive back home and sleep for about a day. Then I cleaned up, checked my bank account, and decided I could afford to take a few days off work for this. Which in my case, simply meant leaving my status as 'unavailable' for my various freelance gigs.

I made appointments with Severino and Arturo for their *despachos*. I wandered into the kitchen to toast a bagel and make a cup of strong coffee, exchange pleasantries with my folks, let them know I was doing *bruja* work, and disappear back into my room—ignoring the now-familiar pinched disapproval on my mother's face and long-suffering bemusement on my father's. I retreated back to my room and dropped into the chair at my desk.

My room is probably not what you would imagine. There's a twin bed in one corner, and a mid-sized desk in another. Other than that, it's just a couple of large bookshelves and a fairly open space in the middle of the floor. The shelves are a disordered riot running the gamut from texts on herbs and nature to radical politics to Indigenous and Latin American history, to stack upon stack of fantasy and mystery novels.

True, my taste in decorations does tend to run toward traditional Peruvian handicrafts. But nothing in the room really cries out 'magic'! There are no pentagrams or crystal balls, no animal pelts or feathered headdresses, no carefully displayed herbs in bundles or in jars. Most of those things would have nothing to do with my work, and those that do are too precious to wave about like tourist souvenirs. My work supplies are kept carefully stored and labeled in plastic tubs on a built-in shelf in my closet.

It's not that I'm a neat freak—just look at my bookshelves. But it's important to me that my workspace stay neat. That includes my desk. The desk is for computer work, and snacks. And thinking.

I was in over my head on this, that was certain. I had no idea what manner of being I was dealing with, but I would bet my car that it had me outclassed in experience, resources, and raw supernatural power.

Look at me. I was basically three-quarters traditional healer and a quarter hedge magician, with a minor in banishing troublesome entities. I was no Dr. Strange, nor Van Helsing, nor even Lew Archer.

But, in for a penny, in for a pound. I'd decided to go after the monster, so Ana María would just have to do.

If the victim had still been alive, I would have started by interviewing him and his entire family, to try and get a sense of how he might have attracted malevolent spiritual attention. It wasn't that different, honestly, from what a detective might do in compiling a list of suspects. But none of that would do me any good here, and not just because I didn't even know who the victim had been. The pishtako hadn't known either, and it hadn't cared. It was an opportunistic hunter. The only thing it cared about was that its victim was an Indian, and alone.

Which meant there was only one way for me to track the monster down: **magic**.

So I got to work building a *mesa*.

The base was a simple card table, which I covered with a traditional Andean carrying cloth, all colors and patterns and stripes. It was hand-woven from llama wool, and I'd had a devil of a time tracking it down.

I placed a scallop shell at the head of the table, with the toenails inside it. Then I spread more shells across the table, each one a place setting filled with sacred foods to attract the right kind of helper spirits and with medicines to protect and guide me in my search.

I pinched off a golf ball-sized lump of ceramic modeling clay, mixed in a little of the mangrove earth the body had been lying on, and molded the mass into a small, manlike shape. I worked carefully for a couple of hours to add the details of hands and feet, with the right number of fingers and toes, and small lumps to represent the genitals. The face I left blank. I said a brief prayer and affixed a toenail clipping to one of the figurine's feet.

Then I took a sharp knife and pruned off its head and hands. The head and hands went into a tiny, burlap wedding-favor baggie that I tied shut. I used the knife to slash shallowly at the neck and the ankles. Then I put the figurine and sack into an empty scallop shell, which I placed alongside the shell containing the remaining clippings.

The anthropologists call this *sympathetic magic*, but I feel frustrated by that concept. It seems somehow condescending: look at how simple minds find connections between *totally separate* things! But hey, what more can you expect from such backward folk? Of *course* they think that spilling water on the ground will bring rain.

As if our spiritual beliefs were simply an exercise in synecdoche and metaphor. Rather than the more obvious truth: synecdoche and metaphor resonate deeply with human beings because *that's how the universe actually functions.*

Yes, I was using the victim's toenail clippings to form a connection with his soul. But certainly not because both soul and clippings had once been connected to a certain body, now dead.

No. The dead body was like a seed, filled with potential. The soul had not fled; it was still there.

It was in the land of the ancestors, too. It's only Western dualism that makes it seem like it should be one or the other.

And the toenails? Well, you *could* say that the part always yearns to reconnect with the whole. But the truth is that there are no separate parts; there is only the whole, seen from many vantages. The nail clippings were like the moon viewed at the end of her cycle. Only the barest sliver of the victim was visible, but all of him was still there.

With the proper prayers and offerings performed, I used Mama Mapacho to call up my healer's sight again. The scallop shell holding the clippings was filled with the same miasma I'd seen earlier—smaller, but no less potent, and just beginning to ooze over the brim. Just a razor-thin crescent next to the fullness of the pishtako's power.

I picked up the shell with the miniature and touched it to the edge of the shell holding the clippings. "This is you," I said. "You are this."

I felt a flow of *camac*, of life force. The miasma exploded from the shell in my hand, sending angry tendrils surging toward my face. An inch away, they shattered against the protection of Mama Mapacho and my other medicines. I frantically chanted protective prayers until slowly, reluctantly, the darkness receded into the shell, where it began to pulse like a beating heart.

My body was drenched in sweat. My mouth was dry. And I was grinning.

The miniature is not a representation of the body: it *is* the body, in a different form. The shell now held the full strength of the victim's dormant life force. More importantly, it held the full strength of the pishtako's spiritual miasma.

I held my quarry's soul in my hands.

———

It had never occurred to me that I might have to deal with the spiritual version of a radioactive isotope, so I didn't exactly have any containment methods ready to go. So I tipped the clippings into the same shell as the miniature, stacked the shells inside each other, and set them carefully in the center of the *mesa*, surrounded by medicines and place settings for protective spirits. Then I set to jury-rigging a lead-lined suitcase.

My 'suitcase' was a clear, plastic pencil case that I purified with *mapacho* smoke and sprinkled with red-and-black wayruru seeds. Then I closed the shells into a gallon-sized ziplock bag, put the bag in the pencil case, and snapped the lid shut. Finally, I slipped a bracelet made from wayruru seeds onto my wrist, just in case.

I took the pencil case out to my car, set it on the passenger seat, and stared at it for a while. I was attuned to the miasma now, and I could see the tendrils of contagion squirming within the plastic bag. From this vantage: the fragment, stretching toward the whole.

Within a minute or two, a clear pattern emerged. Viewed over time, there were many more and larger tendrils pulling toward the southeast.

Well, that was where the body had been found, so that made sense. I'd just have to hope that the miniature would lead me to the pishtako, and not just back to the victim's body.

At this point, you may be asking: Why, if I had hold of the pishtako's soul, didn't I just stay in my room and attack it directly? Because my *abuela* didn't teach me black magic. And even setting aside the dire costs of starting down that path, I certainly had no desire to begin by setting my untrained skill against an enemy whose spirit was this powerful. So tracking it would have to be.

I got on 36th Street and drove east. Right around the airport, I pulled over and checked the tracker again. What I thought of as the compass needle had split into two. A smaller one pulled south, toward Coral Gables. That would make the larger one, still pulling southeast, my line to the pishtako.

By the time I got to I-95, the needle still pointed southeast, toward the Atlantic. I cursed softly and pulled over, then called up a map on my phone. Sure enough: either the pishtako was in the Wynwood neighborhood, or it was out on the Keys somewhere—or worse, on a boat. But I'd cross that bridge—hah!—if I came to it. I drove south on I-95 until I'd passed Wynwood, then checked the tracker again.

Sharp southeast.

Grumbling, I got off the road and pulled up the map again. Now I knew my quarry was either on the islands or out at sea. From my current location, I could rule out Miami

Beach or its neighboring islands. If it was possible to drive to the pishtako, there was only one way to get there.

I got back on I-95 and drove south, then out onto the Rickenbacker Causeway, with the waters of Biscayne Bay shining turquoise and blue below me. The tracker held a steady course past Virginia Key, and within 15 minutes I was pulling into the village of Key Biscayne.

I drove slowly, feeling self-conscious. Key Biscayne is the wealthiest town in Florida. In *Florida*. It's not that my fifteen-year-old, slightly battered Honda Civic made me stand out, precisely, it was just...out of place.

The village looked like the kind of place that should only exist on TV. You know—patently wealthy, but not in an *ostentatious* way. Where every vantage looks on a scene from a postcard. Picture-perfect tropical suburbia.

I did a quick triangulation and followed my tracker toward the bayside coast.

Of course I did.

I finally found it on a street full of seaside mansions, each roughly half the size of a city block. The house was two stories tall, or maybe three, looming over the eight-foot, ivy-covered wall separating it from the plebeian street. A guardhouse sat next to the massive, electric gate that provided the only apparent access.

I drove slowly down the street, eyeing my tracker. The pishtako was definitely somewhere inside that...compound.

My first impulse was to pull over—I hate trying to think while I'm driving. And then it hit me. Here I was, a *chola*, alone, favored prey of a monster, getting ready to park my—yes, *conspicuously low-class car*—in front of its den.

I snapped some photos with my phone, hopefully looking like a mainlander tourist, then drove to a public park and sat under the shade of a palm tree, my hands shaking uncontrollably.

What, in the name of God's green earth, was I supposed to do with *this*?

————

I've always liked puzzles. Jigsaw puzzles, yes, but word puzzles most of all. Riddles and math problems and crosswords and mysteries. It's a big part of what drew me to *abuela*'s work. Figuring out the source of a malady, which *madres* to consult, which herbs and ceremonies to combine for a cure—it was like a giant riddle begging to be solved.

That's how I've always felt about the natural world. I've always just wanted to *know*. What does this animal eat, where does it sleep, and how do all these beings fit together? It's what set me to roaming beaches and swamps while my brother and sister were working hard to carve out a social space in this new country they'd been dropped into.

And of course, the mysteries of the universe are the greatest puzzle of all. Once *abuela* started to teach them to me, I knew that I was hooked. Here was a puzzle that could occupy me for the rest of my life.

So, when I got home from my jaunt to Key Biscayne, I was terrified and daunted, but I also felt angry and stubborn and a little bit of a thrill.

How was I going to crack this one?

I locked myself in my room and sat at my tiny desk, thinking.

I was never getting into that house; that much was obvious. And for all I knew, the pishtako could be anyone in there—a house cleaner, a chauffeur, a cook.

Could be, but probably wasn't. In the stories, pishtakos were men (and occasionally women) of power. Sometimes all that meant was to be a white foreigner with a camera or a syringe. But power nonetheless.

In South Florida? It was whoever owned or lived in that house, or one of their guests.

A reverse address search on the house yielded nothing.

Which brought me to my next question: did it matter who the pishtako was? Someone of that caliber was basically untouchable by someone like me. What was I going to do, trail them in my beat-up Civic? Call in an anonymous tip to the cops and promptly get dismissed as Just Another Florida Crazy?

If I was going to stop the pishtako, I would have to catch it in the act. On the prowl for *cholos* to murder, the pishtako would have to leave most of its social armor behind. It would be as vulnerable as I was likely to find it.

And catching the monster in the act would probably take magic, not mundane sleuthing.

Which suggested that there was no point in digging any further into the killer's identity. I wanted to know; of course I did. But there was no *point*, and there were definite risks in continuing to dig, particularly if it meant going back to that house.

Knowing more isn't always better. I know, I know: the scientists and their followers have elevated knowledge to the status of a benevolent deity. But I was trained in a different path, and I firmly believe that knowledge is only for those with the training and wisdom to use it properly. Sometimes, it really is better not to know.

But better or worse, knowledge *is* power. And right now, I could use all the power I could get.

So I drove back to Key Biscayne at around dusk on the day before trash pickup, and I stole some garbage and recycling out of the mansion's curbside bins.

The only name on the mail was Lucio A. Mendoza. So who was this Mendoza, a man concerned enough about his privacy to have an unlisted name and number, worried enough about his safety to justify an eight-foot wall and armed guards, yet willing to toss mail with his name on it directly into the trash?

Maybe he had no understanding of basic security culture. Maybe it had never occurred to him that his junk mail was a weakness. That seemed...implausible.

Or maybe he simply wasn't worried about concealing his identity from people who were already looking through his trash. That seemed much more likely. After all, he had plenty of physical security to deter anyone who wanted to bother him at home.

And *why* did he have that security, precisely? Key Biscayne wasn't exactly a high-crime neighborhood.

It suggested that he wasn't thinking about a tracker like me, who found his house but had no idea who he was. Instead, he was worried about people who already knew his *name* looking for where to find him.

Well, well.

The top result on a web search for his name and "Miami" was a post by an organization called ¡Abya Yala Resiste! I knew of them—a human rights monitoring and advocacy group that worked exclusively in the Americas.

'Peruvian War Criminals Still At Large', the headline read.

During the height of Peru's armed internal conflict from 1980–2000, between 65,000 and 80,000 people were killed or disappeared. Hundreds of thousands more were displaced, tortured, or forcibly sterilized. The vast majority of those targeted were Indigenous people.

Nearly half the killings and disappearances were perpetrated by government and paramilitary forces. Yet very few of the leaders responsible for these atrocities have ever been prosecuted.

I felt a familiar tightness in my chest and gut. It was a history my family was more than familiar with. I skimmed ahead. The article was mostly a list of former military officials who had been implicated in atrocities but were still at large. And there he was.

Lucio Arturo Mendoza Torres. Believed to be 'El Demonio Jaguar', leader of the Grupo Jaguar military unit. Witness testimonies have linked Grupo Jaguar to war crimes and crimes against humanity.

I read over the allegations, a chronicle of massacres and mutilations, feeling both angry and nauseated at the same time. Neither of my parents' home villages was on the list.

Mendoza retired from the military in the late 1990s and was briefly active in Peruvian politics before emigrating to the United States in 2002. He currently resides in Miami. He is a board member or major investor for numerous companies, including—

A list followed, mostly mining and energy companies. At the bottom of the page were a pair of links urging me to write to the Peruvian Attorney General and to U.S. Immigration and Customs Enforcement and ask them to launch investigations into Mendoza.

I stared at the screen for a long time. I sat very still, turning the options over in my head again and again.

A lot of my social circle were anarchists and radical activists of various stripes. I'd been introduced to them by an herbalist friend of mine and found that we had a lot in common.

Some months ago now, Andrew, the boy I'd kind of been seeing, had insisted on installing a variety of encryption programs on my computer and showing me how to use them. I never had.

Now I took a screenshot of the article on Mendoza, then moved it into a new folder that I named 'Client Information' and encrypted. I cleared my browser history. I emailed myself the encrypted file, then set my computer to do a secure wipe of the hard drive, thereby eliminating all non-encrypted traces of the article. Only then did I pick up my phone and call my dirtbag cousin, Manuel.

"Ana María? What's wrong?" he asked in English.

Fair enough. No one in my family has anything to do with Manuel, except at holidays and reunions. And it was nowhere near Christmas or his mother's birthday.

"The family is OK," I said. "But I need to talk to you. Can you meet me at South Beach, at the corner of Ocean and 5th? Any time of day is fine."

"Is this a joke?"

"More like an emergency. Listen, I just need to talk to someone who doesn't see things the way the rest of the family does."

He was quiet just long enough for my doubts about this path of action to surface all over again.

"All right," he said. "I can meet you there at five-thirty. You just going to be standing in the street?"

"Haha. I'll be at the corner in the park. And thanks."

I got there early. What else did I have to do? And I was afraid that if I delayed, I'd chicken out.

My cousin is...not a nice guy. No, that's unfair. Manuel is actually quite polite to most people, treats his mother very well, and seems to be at least a half-decent father.

But he's not a good person.

Manuel was kind of a mess as a teenager and got himself locked up more than once. The last time, he was carrying just enough cocaine and was just close enough to a school, that he ended up serving a couple of years.

He came out of prison as a sort of enforcer for a gang called Los Cholos Negros. I don't know exactly what he does, but I do know that it seems to pay him well, that he has no other job, and that my mother refers to him as 'that damned murderer'.

I don't know what *he* does. But I know how to use the Internet just fine, thanks, and I have a pretty good idea of what his *organization* does. They have their fingers in every type of lucrative organized crime you'd expect, from smuggling to money laundering to other digital and financial crime. And drugs, of course. Especially illicit prescription drugs; that's where the money is.

The group's name comes, in part, from their practice of dressing in black clothing and ski masks and hacking their enemies to death with machetes.

So yes, I was a little nervous sitting on a bench in Lummus Park and pretending to read the fantasy novel in my lap.

Let's recap, I said to myself. *I've now failed to report a murder, dumped a body in a swamp, stalked a millionaire and stolen his trash, and now I'm meeting with Manuel, of all people.*

There had been a moment, staring at Mendoza's name on my computer screen, when I had considered walking away from this. *Seriously* considered it, in a way that I really hadn't this whole time. It was the logical thing to do. Frankly, there were too many reasons to even list them all.

But something in me wouldn't let this go. Maybe it was the same something that made me apprentice to *abuelita* in the first place, that made me stick with her path instead of doing something more mainstream like becoming an herbalist, or an acupuncturist. That made me embrace the title of *bruja*, instead of the more understated, perfectly respectable *curandera*. The something that keeps me following her rule that people of our sort *never* charge for our services.

Stubbornness? Pride? A sense of responsibility to ancestors long dead?

It came down to this: A monster was killing people. *My* people. Who was going to help them, if I didn't?

So here I was, watching Manuel saunter over, a thickset man of middling height dressed in gray linen slacks and a long-sleeve, white linen guayabera. His clothes were simple and well-fitting in that way that spoke of money. And I was no expert, but I suspected that those were designer sunglasses on his face.

At least he'd had the decency cover his heavily tattooed forearms. It was a concession he never made for family gatherings, and it made me feel a little better about this meeting. He didn't know why I wanted to meet him, so he was making an effort to blend in.

I was making my own effort, in a low-cut, high-hemmed, spaghetti-strap floral sundress, mostly red and black to match my wayruru jewelry. I'd gone all-out on the seeds this time, sporting not only the bracelet but also a necklace and earrings to match. The look was more Beach Hippie than Miami Vice, but either one fit in fine here.

"Ana María," he said, dropping onto the bench next to me. "So you going to tell me what we're doing here?"

"First we're going to your car, so you can leave your cell phone in it," I said. "Then we'll walk."

He stared at me, expressionless behind his dark glasses. He had the same bold nose and cheekbones as everyone I'd been spending time with recently.

"Shit, cousin, what kind of trouble are you in?" But he stood up, and we started walking.

Did you know that it's a simple hack for law enforcement to turn any cell phone into a remote listening device? Look it up; it's true. I didn't believe it either when my anarchist friends first told me.

After locking Manuel's phone in his car, we turned around and headed back to the park. "If you're wearing a wire," he muttered, but I could tell it was mostly for show.

I snorted. "Yeah, wait till you hear my story. It's totally the kind of thing the feds would cook up."

I meant what I said, but I'd still been careful. There was a reason I'd chosen such a sparse dress. I had no pockets, and no purse; my paperback was still clutched in my hand. I figured trust had to go both ways.

"So why are we in South Beach, again?" he asked. The sun was setting, and the streets were filling with the young, the rich, and the on-vacation en route to the restaurants, clubs, and bars. I could just make out the beach on the other side of the park. It looked packed.

"Because this place is filled with tourists and strangers. No one is going to look twice at us, and we're not likely to run into anyone we know."

He shrugged, accepting it. "All right, shoot. I'm dying of curiosity," he said, with such perfect irony that I knew the words must actually be true.

I shoved away my fears and said, "I'm hunting a pishtako. It's been killing immigrants, all *cholos*. I saw one of the bodies."

"You're shitting me," he growled. "What is this?"

I stopped dead and gave him my *bruja* stare, face stern but otherwise completely blank.

He held my gaze for a moment, then looked away.

"Do you think I would make this up, you ass?" I said coldly. "Do you think I would call you to play some kind of *prank*?"

"Shit," he breathed, and I could tell that he believed me. "Shit!"

It was often like this, with people like us—younger, born and raised in the States. Hell, it was like this with older folks, too. People wanted so badly to believe in an empty, rationalist universe.

And there I was, a living wrench in the gears of their Clockwork God.

Gangs of laughing twenty-somethings and couples strolling arm-in-arm surrounded us as we started walking again.

"All right," he said. "So why don't you just...magic it away?"

"Idiot," I snapped. "A pishtako is a human being, not a spirit or a faerie creature. A human being backed by incredible worldly power. You think I have any way to touch someone like that?"

My rudeness seemed to reassure him, putting us back on familiar ground. "Like the Church or the military," he said, nodding. "I remember the stories. So you've found him?"

"I've found him." I sighed. "And there's nothing I can do to him. But you..." I glanced around, saw no one cared at all about us, and dropped my voice anyway. "You have access to guns, and people willing to use them. And I have magic that, I think, can tell me where the pishtako is going to strike next. So if you can bring your people to lie in wait, we can hopefully kill him before he gets his next victim."

To his credit, he thought it over seriously before shaking his head.

"Sorry, *prima*, but no one is going to believe this old-world bullshit. Even the guys that are at church every Sunday or pray to Santa Muerte. If you told them they had a spiritual sickness brought on by *mal aire* and you had to shove a guinea pig up their ass, they'd probably believe you. But you're asking me to order a hit on what sounds like someone rich and respectable. I don't have that authority, and the people who do would never order it based on a campfire story."

I was too used to his affected irreverence to take much offense. "I think they'll authorize it. Do you know the name Lucio Mendoza?"

His easy stride faltered for just a single step.

"Yeah," he said softly. "I know the name. Are you saying it's him?"

I hadn't called Manuel just for his professional resources and moral flexibility. I'd called him because of *who* he worked for.

Los Cholos Negros started out as a neighborhood gang, protecting Black and Brown Latine immigrants from exploitation by cops and other gangs. For all its criminal ventures, the gang still views itself as a protective force.

To what extent LCN actually protects anyone is certainly up for debate—but they *see* themselves that way. In a couple of notorious cases, they've even assassinated police or prison guards who've escaped punishment for egregious brutality. Or so the story goes.

I didn't think they'd pass up a chance to take a shot at Mendoza.

"I *think* it's him. And if my *hechizo* works, it can take us to someplace away from his defenses. I'll point the pishtako out to you, and you kill him."

This time, he was the one to stop walking. He took off his glasses and looked me in the eye.

"Ana María, do you really want to do this? I know you've seen some crazy things, but...well, it's like you said. He's an evil, fucked-up killer, but he's also a human being. I'm guessing you've never done anything like this before. And if I understand what you said, you actually have to be there when it happens? That's...that's fucked. Let it go. Or tell us where you think he'll be and let us go there, and make our own call."

"God damn it, you think I haven't thought about this?"

"I know you haven't," he interrupted. "You've never killed someone, so you don't know what you're talking about. You just think you do."

"Then tell me another way to stop him. Do you have one?"

He gave me that sardonic smile. "And if I did, would you still want me to kill him? I've always said your dad and I are more alike than anyone wants to admit. Maybe you and I are, too?"

I just stared at him. Not my *bruja* stare. Just my *I didn't come here for bullshit* stare.

He shrugged. "Doesn't matter. I'll do it. I'd love to erase that bastard from the earth." He put the glasses back on. "I'll call you from a burner phone at four tomorrow. Get your own—that's a prepaid phone, use cash and don't give them any info about yourself—and call, don't text me, from it when you know when and where. You set this up well, so don't get stupid now. Call from somewhere you won't be heard or watched. Not your house or your car. You know what happens if we get caught."

And then he walked away.

————

Roughly six weeks later, I found myself crammed into the back of an unremarkable-looking, windowless white van, surrounded by heavily armed, black-clad masked men. And I do mean *crammed*; there were at least a dozen gunmen back there, enough that each of my shoulders pressed tightly against those of my neighbors. The men joked easily in Spanglish, bragging about what they'd do to the war criminal when they caught him. It made my stomach do queasy flips. The van was musty with the scent of too many bodies in a too-small, poorly ventilated space.

Much to my appreciation, Manuel had picked me up first—at our agreed-upon location, far from where either of us lived or worked—and let me have the whole van to myself so I could change into the black clothing and ski mask he'd provided, without any strange men gawking at me or seeing my face. Only then had we gone to gather the rest of the men.

I was the only one not holding a weapon; instead, I clasped my hands—clammy within their gloves—tightly together. The pishtako tracker, still in its clear plastic case, bulged in one of the large pockets of my cargo pants. The wayruru bracelet nestled hidden beneath my long sleeves; it hadn't come off since I'd slipped it on my wrist all those weeks ago. Those charms, and the tiny amount of mapacho that remained to me, would have to be weapons enough.

I had no coca leaves; the divination I'd performed had liquidated my precious stash, also burning through nearly all my mapacho and great quantities of other herbs both common and rare. It wasn't just the herbs that had been used up; the ritual had taxed me to my limit—days of round-the-clock work on minimal sleep, fueled by microwave burritos and what seemed like gallons of coffee.

I had borrowed my friend Mari's garage to do it in. My parents would never have stood for me locking myself in my room for days, or for the noxious odors that would have wafted into the rest of the house. Easier to just disappear for a while. The garage at Mari's house served mostly as an untouched storage space. She'd agreed to park her car in the driveway until I was done, giving me a precisely car-sized rectangle to set up my workspace in.

The ritual was like nothing I had ever done, like nothing my *abuela* had ever taught me. It was sheer extrapolation on my part, cobbled together from disparate bits and pieces, from theory and reading and guesswork. But my *abuela* had taught me that the future was like a great river, rushing up from behind us. Sometimes, it was possible to listen through the roar of the current and make out voices.

Power filled the cluttered garage. My technique was sloppy; I could feel the *camac* that I called up spilling off the edge of the *mesa* and filling the room. Then came the slew of guiding spirits I had invoked, one for every herb involved and then some. I couldn't see them, couldn't sense them individually, but I could feel the spiritual pressure of them on my forehead. As the ritual wore on, the garage felt more crowded and the pressure grew worse.

The pressure exploded within my skull, and I wasn't in the garage any longer. I had no body; all I could see was the mangled spirit of the pishtako's last victim. The image was translucent, as if barely present, but the wounds gaping across its body were vivid, and they welled with black contagion. The victim looked even more wasted and shrunken than I remembered of his corpse. The head and hands floated beside the body, just shy of touching where they'd been severed.

Tomás Castro Gutierrez, he hissed without a voice. *Remember me!*

I could not say if the shade spoke English, or Spanish, or another tongue.

Then he was gone, and images were assaulting my mind. An empty parking lot, late at night. A woman returning to her car. A black shadow leaping from the car beside her. A blur of motion. A deserted, run-down apartment complex. The shadowy form stringing her by her ankles, hoisting her…

The memory brought on a shiver, quickly suppressed; I didn't want the men next to me to mistake it for fear. Well, I was afraid, damn it, but that wasn't why I wanted to shiver, and no need for them to think of me as a coward, anyway.

I looked around the van again, trying to distract myself from the details of the vision, that still seared into my mind.

I'd awoken sprawled across the *mesa*, my accouterments scattered across the floor. The headache was worse than ever, along with a thirst that felt like a clawed hand shoved down my throat. But tucked neatly into a corner of my mind was the knowledge, like a pair of addresses in space-time. Where and when the monster would attack next, where and when it would kill.

So here we were, en route to a condemned and supposedly abandoned apartment complex not far from downtown. It was about one-thirty in the morning, and the poor girl from my vision was likely still shopping inside the Walmart Supercenter, or maybe hadn't even started. She wouldn't be back at her car for about half an hour. Then the pishtako would grab her, force her into his car, and drive her here.

And this was where she would die if anything went wrong with our plan.

"We'll be there in five," the driver said, and everyone went quiet.

"You ready, *chola*?" Manuel said.

I wasn't really in a position to challenge his choice of codename, so I just accepted it.

"Ready." I didn't trust myself to use any more words, not without my voice cracking.

"Stick with me," he said, for at least the hundredth time. "The rest of you know what to do."

"Now," the driver said.

The van slowed. One of the Cholos pulled the door open long enough for two others to drop out, then pulled it shut again. The van sped away. I felt us round a corner.

Excruciating minutes passed. Manuel's phone dinged and he glanced down at it.

"All clear," he said.

The van swung us back around and came to a stop. "Everybody out," the driver said.

The night was moonless, black. A slum like this had probably never had a lighted parking lot to begin with, and there wasn't a working streetlight in sight.

The abandoned complex loomed above us, empty doors and windows gaping like the sockets of a skull. It was the building from my vision, that was certain.

"Fuck," I heard one of the men whisper. "I hope our source was legit."

If only he knew, right?

"No talking till we're inside," Miguel hissed. He made for the stairs, and I stuck close behind him. Three of the men peeled away and headed for a unit downstairs.

The complex was what I thought of as motel-style, with each unit having its own door directly to the outside. That meant the staircase was also on the outside, which filled me with no end of relief. I didn't think I could have trusted myself to a staircase on the inside of a place like this. As it was, the handrail was rusted and pitted, but at least the stairs themselves were solid cement.

We went to the apartment next to where the killing would take place. The door was open; I didn't know if the lock had been broken by vandals, or by our scouts. I supposed it didn't matter.

Inside, Manuel parked me in a back corner of what had probably once been a living room, and the men got to work. I watched them for a moment, as they checked their weapons and rigged explosives to one of the walls, but that made my nerves a thousand times worse. So instead, I pulled out my tracker and stared at it. The room was so dark I could barely make out the shadowy figures of my companions. I couldn't even really see the outside of the tracker all that well. But I could *see* the pishtako's miasma, tugging northeast—just as it should.

The miasma no longer pulled toward Coral Gables. As the body had—I assumed—been consumed by the creatures of the swamp and disintegrated into the ocean, its connection with its killer had degraded.

I decided not to care what the other men thought about me staring at a plastic pencil case in the dark—if any of them were even able to see what I was doing. Surely they had their own thoughts, their own problems. Me, I watched the tracker. Manuel came over and crouched next to me, but he said nothing.

Abruptly, the tracker swung west, then south. "They're coming," I whispered.

"Get ready," Manuel said to the room. There was a rustle of movement. "Put your earplugs in," Manuel said to me, by way of clarification.

Right. I fumbled in my pocket until I found them, then stuffed them in through the ear slits of my mask. All traces of sound vanished.

The tracker swung toward the door, and then I heard the purring of a car engine—muted, but still easy to recognize. Should I be relieved that I could still hear, or worried for my ears?

The engine cut off. One of the Cholos crouched by the window, gazing out into the dark. He raised a fist, then three fingers. Then he replaced it with one.

I had no idea what the signal meant, but I supposed the other men did.

Muffled sounds of activity came from outside, the sound of a door opening and closing.

A pinhole of light spilled into the room, through the peephole one of Manuel's team had drilled through the wall—with a sudden shock, I realized that they might have broken into this room and drilled that hole *weeks* ago. Then one of the Cholos pressed his face to the hole and the light vanished.

My heart was pounding, with impatience rather than fear. *So close.* The monster was just on the other side of that wall, and here we sat.

The man at the peephole stood and scurried backward. He raised his hand. Manuel put his hand on my head and gently pushed. Right. I turned away.

There was a clap like God's own thunder and a flash of light that seared through my closed eyelids; for a moment, I was sure I'd been struck by lightning.

Gunfire erupted, seemingly everywhere. Another explosion went off outside, quieter but still loud enough to rattle my teeth. And another, and more shooting. Then the shooting stopped.

I forced myself to open my eyes, and realized I was on my hands and knees, the tracker still clutched in my right hand. I was alone in the room.

There was light coming from the room next door, through a minivan-sized hole in the wall. I lurched to my feet and staggered forward. A hand grabbed my shoulder, keeping me from crossing the threshold. "Stay with me, *chola*," Manuel shouted. My ears were still ringing; I could barely hear him.

Two Cholos were unbinding a convulsing, hooded woman from what looked for all the world like a folding massage table, modified with leather straps for the ankles and wrists. The floor around the table was covered in thick towels, presumably to soak up her blood.

The towels were soaking up plenty of blood, all right, though it didn't look like any of it was hers.

The girl was dressed like someone I might be friends with, in tight jeans and a bright, blousy top—just a young woman going to buy something she hadn't realized she was out of until all the other stores were closed. I wondered why I couldn't hear her making any sound; in her position, I'd be screaming my head off.

My eyes wandered across the rest of the room. The hail of LCN bullets had shredded the opposite wall, leaving a jagged maw about one-third of the way between ceiling and floor. I briefly marveled at the precision of the shooters, keeping their aim high enough to pass over the bound victim while still killing the men who had abducted her.

Those men—three of them—were sprawled on the floor in a mass of blood and gore. Skin ripped away, bones shattered. Their expensive suits had been turned to rags, but their blood-splattered shoes still gleamed a polished black under the light of the Cholos' flashlights.

I tried to feel upset at what I was seeing—it seemed I *should* feel upset, what with my sheltered, middle-class upbringing and all—but I looked at the bodies and felt nothing but satisfaction.

Maybe it was because of all the time I'd spent focused on the tracker, maybe it was the divination I'd done, or maybe my senses were just heightening—but this close, I could feel the evil of the pishtako, like a foul psychic stench wafting from the bodies, tightening bands around my chest and sending a prickling dread along my skin. I shook Manuel's hand off and took a step closer, wanting to see Mendoza's face, to see if it had really been him.

Holygodinheaven.

The shattered face of one of the bodies seemed to be…rippling. It took me a few heartbeats longer to realize that what looked like rippling was bone rearranging itself under the skin, skin knitting back together. A white, gelatinous goo coalesced inside an empty socket, then turned into a dark eye. And then it was Mendoza's benignly plump face, with its carefully groomed mustache and dusky *criollo* tan, and the mouth opened and I saw blood on his teeth and shattered teeth were reassembling and new teeth were pushing their way out of his gums and *he looked directly at me and he smiled.*

Only now did the Cholos realize what was happening, as Mendoza staggered to his feet and put his hand inside his tattered suit jacket. Even my bruised eardrums heard the shouts as the pishtako pulled out what I can only describe as an Uzi. The gun's barrel swung toward me.

Someone hit me from behind with a football tackle, and I collapsed in a painful sprawl, with a crushing weight on my spine. Gunfire exploded again, and screams, and more gunfire.

Then the weight eased and a hand grabbed my shoulder and Manuel was shouting in my ear, "Move! Crawl! Let's go!"

We crawled. The room plunged into darkness again as flashlights fell to the floor. I could feel darkness billowing from the pishtako like smoke from a fire, pressing all the air from my lungs.

We scurried behind the ruins of the wall that had once separated the two rooms. Then we hurled ourselves out the front door of the apartment, and we ran.

————

I followed Manuel's lead, running when he said run, stopping when he said stop. We ditched the masks and gloves in a dumpster that he indicated. Then we ran some more. Finally, we stopped, and he called for a pickup. The same van came to get us.

I spent the night holed up in my room, shivering, replaying the horrid scene over and over.

I had been wrong. Horribly, devastatingly wrong. Just a man, I'd said. So confident! So certain in my knowledge of folk tales that I'd led who knows how many people to their deaths.

What in God's name had that creature been? My mind grappled for explanations, for stories to make sense of it. It found nothing.

The next night, I came down with a searing fever and collapsed in my room. I drifted in and out of consciousness for hours, and I knew that I was dying.

I didn't need a ritual to diagnose what was wrong. After weeks of studying it, manipulating it, trying to contain it, I recognized the twisted heartbeat of the pishtako's corruption at once. I didn't know when or where my defenses had gone wrong; I only knew that I was well and truly caught. I could feel the miasma twining around my soul like an anaconda. I knew how it had to end.

Still, I struggled. I tried calling for help, I tried to make it to the door, but I was too weak to do anything but gasp, wretch, and pass out again. Not that it mattered; I think the only person who could have helped me was *abuelita*, and she was two years dead.

Around dawn, clarity came. I knew it wouldn't last.

I was lying face down on the floor, my own vomit around me. A voice was whispering at me, soft and insistent, from within my *bolsa*.

I tried to stand, and my vision swam. I dry heaved for a moment and then slowly, painfully, crawled over to the *bolsa*. I fumbled in the bottom of the bag, more than half panicked. Who knew how long my lucidity would last?

My fingers settled on a half dozen jagged fragments of dried leaf, and the whispers turned to approving murmurs.

I lifted the fragments carefully to my face, and I almost cried out. Coca leaves, slipped somehow free from their ziplock bag, waiting for who knows how long. Not used up in the divination.

I followed their murmured instructions to the letter, setting up the *mesa* and arranging the needed components with a precision borne from utter terror. I was too weak to waste time wrestling the card table, so I spread the tablecloth directly on the ground. My hands shook so badly that it took me three tries to get my supply box open. I performed the *despacho* for myself, still half-delirious, and when it was done I sprawled on my bed and slept.

When I woke again at noon, the sickness was gone without a trace.

I sat up with that peculiar blend of weakness and strength that you only get after you've been seriously ill. I took a deep breath and swung my legs around to the floor.

Ana María.

I frowned. The soft voice was coming from my box of medicines, still open, next to the remains of the *mesa*. But the coca leaves had truly been used up this time. And I wasn't sick anymore.

I crouched next to the box.

Ana María.

Ana María.

Ana María.

My jaw didn't quite drop, but my mouth absolutely hung open for a moment. The whispers had come together, overlapping. A spondylus shell, a piece of lapis lazuli, and a sling woven from llama wool had just called my name.

I braced myself and picked up the sling, draping it over my palms. It sang softly to me in a voice deeper than language, in image as much as sound. Rituals and secrets teased at my consciousness, flashes of paths I could walk, things I could learn to do.

Shaken, I set the sling down and picked up the spondylus. The smell of ocean air; flashes of sea breezes and cold depths. The shell murmured promises of knowledge to be gained.

That was too much. I fled from the room and immersed in a scalding shower, scrubbing at the sweat and vomit as if I could scour away the last two months.

With my head buried under the faucet, I realized what else was different. My body still felt weak from the sickness, but my spirit felt...*strong*, and growing stronger. The best way I could describe it was as if some external power were flowing into me.

I got out of the shower and braved my room long enough to throw on some clean clothes. A chorus whispered at me from the open box, but I refused to listen. I hurried for the kitchen and made myself some food.

I ate at the kitchen table, staring blankly out the window. My parents were at work, and the house was empty. I could still feel the power growing within me.

I needed time to think. I needed a walk.

I walked briskly, on edge, worried that any car might abruptly disgorge a posse of undercover cops, or men in expensive suits ready with a black bag to throw over my head.

I told myself I was being irrational. If the cops wanted me, they would just come to my house. There was nothing to stop Mendoza from doing the same thing.

This did not make me feel any better.

A voice, languid and enfolding, called to me from the depths of the canal beside the road.

Feeling harassed, I made an about-face. Back home, I carefully packed away my supplies and cleaned up my room. I could still hear the whispers, seductive in their promises.

I binge-watched Netflix. I ate in my room. I didn't answer my phone. I did some online interpreting and risked one brief trip to the grocery store.

Spirits of the dead were gathering around me. They lingered at the edges of my vision but were never there when I turned to look. But I could hear them. Unlike the other voices, these made requests, things that needed to be set right. But they offered things, too. Power and knowledge.

Whatever was happening to me, it showed no signs of slowing. The power grew within me. Ceremonies that, a few short weeks ago, would have been forever out of reach now lay just within my grasp—this I knew, deep in the fat of my middle—if only I could find someone to teach me. If I were willing to trust any of the spirits and tutelaries crowding around me, offering me knowledge.

I knew my isolation was making my mental state deteriorate. Beset by spiritual forces, cut off from human contact, brooding over who might be coming to kill me— my sleep, appetite, and nerves were shot to hell.

But it gave me one thing at least, and that was time to think. And with thinking came clarity over what was happening to me.

I had brushed the land of the dead and returned a changed woman. Something within me had come awake.

Maybe it had been my near death from the pishtako's corruption. Or maybe it had happened earlier, when all those people were dying around me, their spirits hurled shrieking and unprepared into the next life. I could almost still feel the power of life and death that had crackled through the room that night, thrashing my soul like a palm tree in a storm.

Or maybe I had been meant to die from the pishtako's bullets, and my cousin had cheated destiny by saving me.

So now I was different.

It was Manuel who finally pulled me out of my seclusion about a week later, convincing me to meet him at a park not far from my house. I was persuaded not so much by his promise of news as by the simple, overpowering need to be in the presence of someone else who had been there on that horrible night.

Being outside still made me jittery. I actually panicked when a plain, black sedan pulled out of a parking spot. I didn't breathe again until it had driven away.

It was a perfect tropical spring morning, warm and breezy. Birds sang in the trees. A hummingbird hovered in front of me for a full two minutes, whispering an invitation. Then Manuel came walking up and it zipped away, wings whirring.

"Hey, *bruja*," my cousin said, dropping onto the bench beside me. His outfit was nearly the same as the last time we'd met, except that the slacks were brown and the shirt short-sleeved. "Phone is in the car. You really should let me take you out for drinks, instead of talking in a park like this. We survived. That's something to celebrate."

"How many?" I asked.

He sighed, low and deep. "Three others made it out. One of them had a bullet in his side, but he'll live."

"The girl?" My voice cracked.

He shook his head.

I closed my eyes, feeling hot tears.

"Listen," he said after a minute. His voice was quiet and serious. "What we lived through was...well, words don't really cover it, do they? Maybe it's the kind of thing you know more about than I do.

"But I do know how the fear can eat at you, after your first shooting. And you don't need that, not on top of everything else. So do yourself a favor, and don't worry. We had a cleanup crew there before sunrise. Even if someone heard something and called the cops, there'd be nothing there for them to find. And who's going to call? Mendoza sure as hell won't. There aren't any neighbors, and anyway it's not the kind of neighborhood where people try to get more involved when they hear shooting. Mendoza used that spot for a reason."

I didn't say anything, so he kept talking.

"The main thing I wanted to let you know is this: Mendoza's gone. Packed up and moved to LA. His house went on the market this morning."

That got my attention.

"He's moved? You're sure?"

Manuel nodded stoically. I dug my fingers hard into my forehead, feeling angry.

Now he was well and truly beyond my reach.

Did I have even the slightest idea of how to stop him, now that my only plan had failed? No. But there had to be *some* way. Every creature has its weakness.

Obviously, Mendoza agreed. He hadn't gone into hiding; he wasn't afraid that I would *expose* him. He was afraid I might be able to kill him.

Well, there was no chance of that now.

And damn it, it wasn't as if having the pishtako a continent away made me feel any safer. A man with his money and resources could reach out and snuff me as easily from Los Angeles as from Key Biscayne.

Yes, I'd worn a mask that night. But the pishtako had looked into my eyes. He'd *smiled* at me, smiled in a way that made me feel like he *knew* me.

My conversation with Manuel sort of petered out after that. Eventually, he left me with more reassurances that no one was coming for us. Get on with my life, he said. Talk to a priest or therapist, if I had to. Most of all, don't worry.

I stayed on the bench, thinking about the death of the person I had been.

I had always felt like a normal woman before—I just knew how to do some things that others couldn't. Yes, *brujería* came somewhat naturally to me, but I still had to work hard at it.

I just had the knack. That's what my *abuela* had always said. I was the only one of my siblings with the knack.

Now I wondered, the knack for what? Because in the depths of my bowels, I knew: I wasn't a simple *bruja* anymore.

Whatever I was, I would have to figure it out. Because Manuel was right. Eventually, I would have to go on with my life. People were depending on me, people no one else was able—or willing—to help.

And sooner or later, someone would need me for more than just an herbal cure or a complementary treatment. They would need my help with a spiritual sickness. Or a monster.

But the new me couldn't cure anyone, not in the state I was in. The walls I was putting up to keep the voices at bay would also keep out the *madres* I needed to do my work.

The walls were there because I was afraid. But when all was said and done, I was more angry than I was afraid.

So. So. Angry.

That monster had gotten away, and he would go on doing what he did until somebody stopped him. I had tried, and he had handed me my ass on a platter.

Maybe it was time to level up.

I looked into the nearest tree and found the hummingbird perched there, still watching me. I extended an arm.

"*Ven acá, qinti,*" I said.

She flew down at once and perched on my finger.

And we began to make a deal.

© 2022 Daniel Delgado

Fantasy - 11859 words

About the Author

Daniel Delgado (he/him) is a Quechua and Jewish writer, editor, and activist living on O'odham and Pascua Yaqui land in the so-called Arizona borderlands. When he's not at a desk, you might find him growing Native crops in his family's backyard farm, or out exploring the desert. You can also find him on Twitter, **@DDelgadoVive**.

Home Bound

Melanie Bell

"I need someone to take the house, so I can die."

My great-grandmother's voice carried over my parents' creaky landline. "What?" I wondered if I'd heard her wrong, if the static had interfered and my mind had distorted her words into something else.

"Do you want it?" she asked.

"The house?" I'd only seen it once—an ancient stone thing in England, neither modern nor heating efficient, so very drafty and so very big. None of my friends could afford a house. And here I was, a ramen-eating freelance programmer, being offered one.

The bad connection distorted her laugh to a cackle. "What do you think I mean, the kitchen table?"

I placed one hand over the other and pinched the knuckles. The sensation reassured me this was real.

I wondered if this family matriarch, hardy enough to outlive her children and chop her own wood past 100, had contracted some ailment she'd failed to tell us about. Or perhaps she was just old and estate planning.

"I'll take good care of it once you're gone."

My father chuckled when he heard about the phone call. "She's been trying to pawn that place off on everyone. What would you want to move to England for?" Implicit in his tacit disapproval was the thought, *Your family is right here.*

"The UK has the NHS, Dad. I wouldn't have to worry about insurance costs or insulin or inhalers, or any of that. And my work is all remote."

Mom nodded at my logic. I figured she'd bring Dad around like she usually did.

I'd miss my friends, but a change of scenery might be exactly what I needed to bring some dignity into my sad life. The house had been offered. He wasn't going to stop me.

————

I'd expected that phone call to be the end of things for a while, but instead, a plane ticket arrived in the mail.

Living in the States, I rarely had occasion to use my second, British passport, a legacy from my father's side of the family. There was only one stamp in it, from the time I'd gone to France. A summer college course, mostly an excuse to hang out in cafes, drink house wine, and check out French girls; the customs agents had given me odd looks due to the mismatch between accent and passport, but they'd treated me better for it too. I used that passport for my flight to England, a long stretch of dozing and movies.

I was tired and shaky from the journey, my blood sugar low, my airway aggravated. I sat in the airport sipping blackcurrant juice and eating a Cadbury Dairy Milk bar, treats I couldn't get at home, until my legs felt solid beneath me again and my breath flowed with ease. A quick train journey away from London got me to a bare train station where red paint peeled. A few elderly Brits in subdued coats walked the streets with shopping bags, keeping their distance from one another. The town's little houses, mostly brick, had seen better days. This place was no tourist haven of thatched cottages. A lonely billboard advertised McDonald's new cheap coffees.

Twenty minutes down the road, the houses thinned out, not unlike the hairlines of the men I'd seen in the train station—unfortunate men my age or only a little older. Bigger plots of land rambled around me, including a fenced one covered in sheep. "Baa," I called out to them. One or two raised their heads and gave me the side-eye. None answered.

"Am I in the right place?" I asked looking at the map app on my phone. Too many years, you see. Last time, I'd been little enough to hold Mom's hand. She'd be called Mum here.

"Please repeat the question," the assistant app piped up. "I don't understand."

I grumbled and turned it off. I'd meant only to talk to myself.

I wandered down some dead ends, past half-fallen barns and heaps of stone, and eventually found the house-shaped heap of stone I remembered. Last time, it had been raining. Now eerie blades of sun illuminated all the tilted grey house's crevices and cracks. A short gravel path led to the road, and an overgrown, browning field sprawled in back of it, peppered with stands of gorse, bordered by half a stone wall or so that delineated the boundaries of the neighbors' properties. No sheep grazed here, though it would likely benefit from a few.

What are you getting into, Beth? I asked myself. *This thing looks like it needs renovations. Where are you going to get the money for renovations?*

From the will, I suppose. Let's hope there's a will.

I was still fretting about money when the door opened as if in anticipation of my knock. I don't know what I expected from Great-Grandma. A senile old lady bound to the sofa? Instead, she greeted me from the door of the house I was set to inherit with barely a hunch.

"Did you have a safe journey, love?"

Her accent was grittier, earthier than those on the BBC. I lacked the background to know where it came from or what it meant exactly, only that it wasn't posh.

"It wasn't bad, I guess. Good to see you." I bent forward and swept her into a hug. She nestled against my chest, all sharp angles.

"You've gotten so much bigger than me, dear." She laughed. "I have tea and biscuits ready. Let's sit down and talk of death."

A sunray swept across her bone-white hair.

"OK," I shrugged. "I brought a suitcase."

"Guest room to the right. Your room, but not for long. Soon you'll have any one you like."

I followed her as she bounced down the hall, opened the guest room door, and fussed briskly with kettle and cups in the kitchen. "You seem good, Great-Grandma. Lots of energy."

She fixed me with a bright-eyed stare. "Yes, I know. As long as I'm here, I've got bounds and bounds. The house feeds me well. But all my friends are dead, and I'm getting tired of it. Do you take sugar?"

"I'm sorry to hear that," I said, awkwardly settling myself on the sofa.

"Yes. Well. I'm sorry to hear that too. And I know people in your generation aren't doing so well with generational wealth. It's not that they don't respect it. It's that they don't have it. But if you still want it, you're welcome to my home. You can be one of the lucky ones."

"I appreciate it." I gazed from open space to open door, assessing where a work desk might go, admiring the surprisingly decent state of the kitchen with its herb-jar-topped brick fireplace. "That won't be for a while, will it?"

She scrunched her eyebrows together, deepening the lines between, and took a big glug of tea before answering.

"Put down your biscuit and let me show you something."

I followed my sparrow-framed elder down the hall, past faded green wallpaper and paintings of ducks. She opened a door with a brass knob.

"You want to show me an empty closet?" I asked, staring at the dusty shelves.

"It's not empty." She crawled inside, leaving me to wonder if dementia was indeed creeping in, and positioned her body under the bottom shelf. "Come in, put your ear somewhere—the wall will do—and listen."

I shrugged and obeyed. Ear to the wall. Immediately, I yanked it away.

The wall made a rhythmic sound, pumping steadily like a drumbeat or heartbeat. This wasn't the usual hum of plumbing. It boomed.

I pressed my side against the plaster and felt the rhythm vibrate against me.

This couldn't be good. I thought wildly, illogically of Poe—had she murdered someone? Was their heartbeat a sign of dastardly deeds?

It had to be some weird electrical thing, right?

A hand patted mine. I winced; it was only Great-Grandma. "There's no need to be afraid, love. The house's heartbeat takes care of me."

"What?"

"You know my many-times-great-grandfather built this house."

"Yeah?"

"He put a piece of his soul in there, to get it done. Ever since, this house has been...protective. It's cared for its own, bonded with them." She placed a hand over her own heart, an endearing gesture even as a chill crept down me, hair to rising hair. "The people who choose this house, we stay. We care for it, we stay close. Even a few vacation days can be too much for it sometimes, you understand— it has ways of calling us back. We're its family. We give it our energy, our life, and it keeps us vital."

"Wait, you mean literally?" I pictured her bouncing around the grounds, sprightlier at her age than I was in youth.

She stood and bent towards me, taking my firm hands in her paper-fine ones. "It's a bargain, you see. We can't die until a committed member of our line claims the home. The house won't let us."

"So you can't just sell it?" I said, feeling suddenly weak—though my blood sugar was fine.

She snickered. "I don't think the house knows or cares about the exchange of money. But it knows blood. It can come to know our loved ones, grow to protect and mesh with them. But the home bond starts with one of us."

I wondered whether to believe her. Her words were outlandish, her countenance sane. It was the house itself that answered my doubts.

Once we left the closet, the halls opened up to me. The wallpaper rustled. The kitchen cupboards clicked. I swear the dishwasher winked with its blinking lights.

I still wanted that house.

I let Great-Grandma lead me through each room and introduce me, bidding me to touch walls and sniff waxy floors. When we came to a wide room with a gnarl-legged couch, she gestured to the floor again. "You'll sleep here tonight. I'll get you some blankets, and the house will get to know your scent."

My dreams swirled with ghosts and sheep and sheep ghosts. I woke to silence. A frail figure lay on the couch under a blanket she'd knitted herself, glassy eyes open, completely still.

————

"Bad luck," said anyone who heard the coincidental timing of Great-Grandma's death. "She lived a remarkable life. She was very old."

They'd be saying those things about me someday.

I settled things back in the States and moved my life to a country where I'd spent very little time. Speaking earned me strange looks. My friends and parents were several time zones away. There was family over here, at least in name—a distant great-aunt and uncle, some cousins several times removed, friendly but not familiar, with mannerisms and senses of humor so terribly different from mine. I took to long walks and hung out at coffee shops, the coffee defying my expectations by tasting just as good on this side of the pond.

The house needed less work than I'd thought. The morning after I'd decided to replace the holey gutter, I went outside and could no longer find the holes. Roof shingles renewed themselves. The tilt straightened. It still looked ancient, but it always managed to just get by. Not that it saved me, or the first Roomba to roam the splintery corridors, any cleaning.

Sometimes I ended a WhatsApp call across time zones in tears because I couldn't go back, wouldn't ever live in the States again where my accent was normal and the jokes made sense and burgers were pleasantly huge. If one of my parents got sick, I couldn't care for them. I was stuck in this old stone box.

The house creaked, trying, I think, to reassure me. Its heartbeat thrummed steadily in the walls, and I realized I hadn't had a single asthma attack since I'd entered that closet.

I expected the house to be haunted, but no spectral relatives showed up. The only sentience in the house, besides me, was itself. The more responsive it became, the more I began to think of it as an AI, processing my cues and outputting smart responses developed by a type of cognition beyond my own. It preceded computers, but it presaged them.

It was easier to think of it that way than to think of it as magic.

I tested the waters with Great-Aunt Violet, helping her make a roast for Sunday dinner. "Have you spent much time in, uh, my new house?"

An involuntary shiver sped through her. "We don't like it much. Sorry, love, I know it's nice for your work. But none of us wanted that poor old house. I'm glad you took it."

I didn't get much further than that (though the roast dinner was, as my great-aunt put it, 'lovely'). If they knew of the house's eerie properties, clearly my relations would have nothing to do with them.

————

I took my questions to the second-nearest coffee shop, the one with the good flat whites where I worked when I wanted a change of pace. The one, to be honest, with the cute barista.

Tamsin was petite and elfin, with a dyed-black pixie cut, dangling jewelry, and loose bohemian blouses. She beamed and greeted me whenever our work shifts coincided and topped everything that had foam with an artful heart, bird, or flower. She was one of the few women in the UK who didn't call me 'love'. It made sense given her generation, but I kind of wanted her to.

"Any plans for the weekend?" she chirped over (you guessed it) my flat white.

"Just hanging out at home." I paused. "Have you ever been in a house that's seemed like it had a mind of its own?"

Her eyes sparkled as she leaned toward me. "No, but I'd like to see one."

————

The house was on its best behavior for her visit, straightening its roof, shining its windows, sporting white and yellow flowers in the yard I'd dutifully mowed. "How pretty!" she exclaimed over the attic beams and ancient fireplace.

I offered her tea, with homemade scones even. Digging in the kitchen cupboards, I'd found Great-Grandma's recipe file, which I swear I hadn't seen there before.

On our fifth date, I showed her the heartbeat. She reacted like a woman used to fairies and invocations.

"You do realize you're going to have to stay in this house," she told me. "You can't move. Can't go anywhere for long. Can't really escape."

"There's a trade-off for everything," I said. "And my health has been doing better over here. My blood sugar's steadier, though it could be the climate."

She snorted. "That's the first praise I've ever heard for this rainy weather. I doubt it."

I shrugged.

"My plan is to travel the world," she said and showed me pictures on her phone from backpacking across South America.

So while she and I grew closer, enjoying coffees and lantern-lit nights, she never moved in. She used her vacation time in Rome, Snowdonia, Berlin, Sydney, Taipei. The most I did was accompany her on a weekend to Whitstable, where my blood sugar acted up and I dreamed of welcoming walls. When she slept at my place, she kept her eyes on the door. Whenever she whispered "I love you," I heard the unspoken "but."

We kept up our ping-pong relationship all through the first year, while I got used to a flush of energy and pretended it came from the climate. We kept it going through the second year, when my business bloomed and I established a workout room in the basement to explain the hardening of muscles.

And through the third year, when the pandemic struck my adopted country and abandoned homeland alike.

A rambling house is a fortunate place to isolate. While my friends filled social media with photos of fat bread loaves and Zoom dance parties between the four walls of their tiny apartments ('flats' here), I had a whole suite of wood-floored rooms where sunlight caught the dust. I could sit in the yard (a 'garden' here, though nothing but grass and wild growth was planted in it) and soak in fresh air, or run laps around the house, without getting close enough to measure the two meters required for social distancing with my eyes.

————

Tamsin was not so lucky. Her coffee shop stayed open too long, or the rule of masks was implemented too late, or someone got too close with their grubby diseased hand, or something. *Something—*

See how the word reaches out with that little dash, grasping.

It wasn't me who took her to the hospital, but someone else. I wasn't allowed in to see her. Young and healthy, she was given one of the ventilators. I tried not to think too hard of the many who were denied one, the lottery of lives weighed and measured.

The walls of the house tightened around me. I couldn't get out, couldn't leave if I wanted to breathe, keep my sense of taste and smell, avoid droplets in the air. The home pumped in energy, vigor, that compelled my body to move, but it could go nowhere.

I called Tamsin's family for updates. With each day she drifted further from recovery. I should have told her to stay home at the first inkling of virus news. I should have taken her between my own stone walls, ordered grocery delivery, tied her to the bed, forbidden her, like a mad attic wife, from leaving. But what could I do now?

It occurred to me that our last words were a fight over weekend plans, terribly stupid and bitter as coffee grounds. I bit the side of my cheek. I punched the heartbeat's closet. A chunk of peeling plaster fell off and thunked on the ground.

I held it to my angry ear and listened to a faint thump within, a small piece of the house's vitality contained in this part. I pondered.

Tamsin might kill me for this, she who longed to travel, to live always with an exit plan—she who wanted to be with me, yes, but fought for freedom above all else.

But also, she might die.

I seal the plaster inside a clean white envelope, licking it closed. I pray its strength will be enough. That she will hear the tiny imprint of a heart in this shard of home. That she will sit up from her ventilator and freely breathe. That she will always wonder, as she curses me within these halls, whether her life was prolonged by medical competence or by the ties with which I'd bound her.

© 2022 Melanie Bell

Fantasy - 3107 words

About the Author

Melanie Bell is a Canadian multi-genre writer living in the UK. Her books include a short story collection, *Dream Signs*, a nonfiction title, *The Modern Enneagram*, and the forthcoming YA novel *Chasing Harmony*. She has written for several publications including *Contrary*, *Cicada*, *The Fiddlehead*, and *Huffington Post*. She loves music, art, and nature, and aspires to see as much of the world as she can. Find her online at http://inspireenvisioning.com/ and **@InspireEnvision**.

Bleed A Little While

Michael James

Before the world collapsed, they did a poll about the Challenger explosion to determine how many people saw it in their classroom. Eighty percent responded they had clear memories of watching it live.

I remember the grainy images on the TV, watching in rapt attention as the teacher cried in the corner with her hands over her mouth, all of us shocked to silence by the tragedy of the explosion. The memory is so vivid, I can almost smell the cleaning solution they used on the floors.

Someone did the math to figure out how many schools existed in 1986 and further, how many of them had TVs. They determined that if every single TV in every single school had been used, only something like thirty percent of people could have seen it live.

So, did I see it? Or do I remember stories from other people?

Memory was broken even before the Bleed.

————

I don't wear my band around Jeff anymore. Our memories are so blurred, it seems pointless. Besides, they use a ton of energy and it's better to save them for emergencies. Or for days like today.

He kissed me when he woke up and his stubble grated against mine, two pieces of sandpaper rubbing together. I wasn't gay before, but I have so many memories of being with Jeff, that it's hard to remember who I found attractive before the Bleed fused everyone's memories.

When the virus hit, we'd hidden with our wives, all four of us clotted together in the basement. I have clear memories of Jeff asking me to marry him, and the delirious joy of the moment. I remember panting, sticky nights, laughing at his jokes and holding his hand when his sister died. I have the same memories of his dead wife. Or my dead wife? It's hard to tell which memories are pre-Bleed and which came after. Regardless, I remember loving this man and feeling attraction for him, and so here we are. Personality is nothing more than the stories we tell ourselves.

I kissed him back and a small amount of his morning dripped into my brain. I'd woken up and gone for a walk around the periphery of the farm, checking on the fences; Jeff had slept in. Only now that we were close by, I could remember both things and I wasn't honestly sure which one I did. Did I walk the fence? I'm making breakfast, so surely, I didn't sleep in?

I bit my lip and he noticed.

"I slept in, Cooper. I wrote myself a note when I first woke up. See? It's okay."

He showed me the note and I sighed in relief. So, I did walk the perimeter. Even though I remembered sleeping in, I knew which one was fake. Over time, if I cared to, I could force the false one away, but for something like sleeping in, it wasn't worth the effort. He knew how much it bothered me though, and it was dear of him to give me comfort.

"I have to go to town today," I said.

Jeff frowned and took a breath through his nose. "Okay."

"My band is at full power. I'll be safe."

"Yeah. I know."

He didn't like me going out. I hated it too. We lived on the outskirts of Moncton, one of the very few unblurred cities that remained. The virus swept through the larger cities with such incredible speed that no one had any time to react. In a week, all of New York, all eighteen million people, shared amorphous memories of each other's lives, all of them equally real. We were lucky to be in Canada, where the spread-out population gave us some time to protect ourselves.

They made the bands in about three months. Tons of people thought it was a hoax. How is it possible, they reasoned, to come up with protection against this virus so quickly? As it turns out when you focus the accumulated wealth and intellect of seven billion people towards a singular problem, it's not only possible, it's inevitable.

The bands stopped the memory bleed and made the virus tolerable. It didn't cure it; nothing could do that. But at least we could carve out lives. Sort of. As long as you didn't think too hard about who you were and how much of what you remembered was real, it was a life.

We had a list of the basic supplies we needed by the front door. Things like nails, soap, Tupperware if I could find any, aspirin, any long-term foodstuffs.

"I'll go this time," Jeff said.

"You went last time. It's my turn."

"Are you sure?"

I paused. I could clearly recall both going and staying home. The notepad we kept hung on the fridge was filled with dates, notes, little reminders. Writing was infallible. Memory was a liar.

"Don't do that. We wrote it on the list. See? Next turn: Cooper."

"I'm only worried about you."

"It will be fine. In and out."

We grew potatoes because they were stupidly easy to grow. About a year ago, we'd done a memory swap with our neighbour. He'd grown up on a farm and knew everything there was to know about crops. Jeff was a doctor. The three of us got together and took off our bands, and boom. Now we had memories of how to work a farm, and he knew how to suture a wound. On the downside, we also remembered another dead spouse, another childhood, another life, and so on, but the price was worth it.

I'm not entirely positive, but I think I have nine people's worth in my head. Jeff has maybe ten. We were lucky. Some people, like in the cities, have millions. No wonder so many people chose to end it.

There was no sense in putting it off, and so I loaded up the bike with potatoes, kissed Jeff goodbye and stopped for a long hug that I enjoyed very much. Jeff had never been one for hugging, probably his wife's memory, but I also remembered how badly Jeff wanted to be hugged, perhaps a memory from Jeff himself. Who knew? Our brains only recall the information, not where it was gathered. Research papers with no footnotes.

The risk of going to a city is if your band malfunctions, or someone knocks it off, or any of one hundred other things that could go wrong. Moncton wasn't too bad; it had a band mandate. You could get in and out without losing yourself.

———

The walls appeared on the horizon, a slapdash construction that surrounded the city, rising to as high as a hundred feet in some parts and as low as ten in others. The lineup wasn't bad, but my stomach clenched as I approached. My band heated immediately, already hard at work. Nothing could stop the virus from transmitting, so all the bands did was destroy new memories before they had time to take root. The burning I was experiencing was wiring in my brain being microwaved. The less time I spent here, the better. My headband was an older model and it would get hot enough to almost burn the skin. Sweat already dripped down my cheeks, but I tightened the straps.

I really hated the bands.

Passage through the wall only required proof your band was running, and the line moved quickly. It conjured the memory of waiting for two hours to get a marriage license, and a companion one of registering online in five minutes. I wish I knew which one was mine. With no way to tell, I picked the memory I liked best, and let that one win. Sort of how everyone did it before, except now we all acknowledged it.

I traded exclusively with Nora, not only because she had the best selection, but because she was closest to the wall. As a bonus, both Jeff and I found Nora to be affable and honest, so there was no conflict when our dual memories of our visits with her merged.

When I went inside, Nora was arguing with a customer, yelling at them to get out. The guy's face was flushed red, and he pointed his finger at her while he hollered some choice swear words. I wasn't sure if the guy was going to get violent, so I made my way to the counter in case Nora needed help. But the guy turned with his head down and shouldered past me, slamming the door on the way out.

I tried to grin, to make light of it. "What was that all about, Nora? Haven't I seen that guy in here before?"

She ran her fingers through her hair, breathing deeply. "Sorry, Cooper. Yeah, he used to shop here. We were soaked into each other."

"Then why the scrap?" It was somewhat unusual to fight, or even get angry, with someone you'd shared memories with. Once you understood every decision they made as if you made it yourself, it tended to make you more forgiving.

"I remember what he did, but it's not me anymore. I can't believe I allowed that in my head for so long."

"What?" I was having trouble following what she was telling me.

"The new headbands." She tapped the one on her head and her eyes shone with excitement. "God, haven't you done it yet? This is the new upgrade, just released yesterday. I'm surprised no one came by your farm. They have people out all over the place, basically giving these away for free."

"What's the big deal? Less heat?"

"No, Cooper, they cut out all the memories that aren't yours."

"What?"

"They finally did it. They figured out a way to eliminate any foreign memory." Nora smiled beatifically. "It's just me in here, Cooper. It got rid of everything else. It works." She reached behind the counter and handed me a band.

"Are you serious?" I took it from her and turned it over in my hands. "It takes away everything?"

"It's almost over Cooper. Once these get out and people put them on, we can go back to normal. They're already talking about a version that can be implanted permanently. Here, you can put it on right now. They told me to pass out as many as I can, I have dozens."

I hesitated. If this thing worked as Nora said, it would mean my pre-bleed memories of Jeff would vanish. I'd still remember being with him, but what would that mean? How would I feel about him if all my memories of us disappeared? Did I even want that? Would I still love him if I were only me? I didn't want to stop being in love with him.

I took two headbands and got the rest of the stuff and finished up as fast as possible. I'd need to talk to him about this. Whatever we did, it needed to be a decision made together. Surely, I'd still love him. We had two years of memories together that wouldn't be erased, they belonged to us exclusively. Surely that would be enough.

———

When I got home, Jeff was sitting on the porch, like he always did around this time of day. He liked to have 'moments of reflection' as he called them, even though I knew he mostly just liked to fall asleep in the sun.

Something sparkled on his head as I approached and I realized he was wearing his headband. He never wore his headband. My stomach dropped.

It was the new model.

I stopped in front of the porch, and he stood up. Neither one of us moved, we only stared at each other from across the space.

"You put it on," I finally said.

"Cooper—"

"Why didn't you talk to me about it? I waited for you, see?" I held out the two new bands. "Why didn't you wait?" My heart was beating so fast I could hardly hear anything. I wanted so badly for him to reach out to me. I knew he loved being hugged. Why wasn't he hugging me?

He gave me the sad eyes that meant he was upset about something and said, "We should talk."

I shook my head and stepped forward. "Take off your headband and let's merge. We can still work."

"No, Cooper, stop."

I ripped off my headband and lunged at him, but he skipped out of the way. With my headband off, all his memories slammed into mine.

His hands, reaching up to put on the new headband. The sensation of all the corrupted memories being peeled away, like stripping paint off a wall. Seeing myself, through his eyes, the disgust for what we'd done. Relief, now that he could think clearly, that he was free of me.

All of this became my memory, leaving me with remorse and regret. I remembered thinking how I'd forced us to bleed, but no, that wasn't the way it happened, we did it together, a joint decision. But Jeff was telling himself new stories now and they were all becoming my stories.

I dropped to my knees and looked up at the man I loved, who did not love me back. All of the happy times we'd spent together were being replaced with rage for what I had done. I'd forced this on him, apparently the only story he could tell himself that would let him go on.

"Put it on, Cooper." He kicked the new band over. "It's better. I promise."

A wave of self-loathing so profound that I shook with the hurt of it tore through my body. I picked up the device. What choice did I have? I still loved him. And he didn't even like me.

Perhaps, in time, I wouldn't remember this moment at all.

I put the band around my head.

© 2022 Michael James

Science Fiction - 2381 words

About the Author

Michael James is the Canadian author of the fantasy series, The Hotel at the End of Time. His work has been featured in several anthologies, including "The Website is Broken" in *Executive Dread*, and "Attention" in *Horror Library Volume 7*. He can be found on Twitter **@MikeJamesAuthor**

Stasis

Lucy Zhang

There are two rules of this world: one, everything reverts to its original state which means our injuries vanish shortly after getting hurt and our food supply restocks itself daily; and two, we cannot escape alone. We've been here for two weeks now: me, Junlan, and the rest of the class who happened to be on the track field the moment our surroundings vanished, leaving only the grass and polyurethane and the school building. They've been theorizing how to go home, trying to jump off the edges of our bounded plane into what appears to be empty space only to reappear back next to us, trying to overdose on sleep meds in hopes that dying might let them escape. They should know better; we can't die here. There's some kind of balance that must be maintained, the same way matter can't be destroyed. I spend most of my time in the library, where I lie down on the carpet, staring upward at the array of lights and stained-glass windows. Junlan asks me why I'm wasting time doing nothing, but the joke is on him, because I suspect time isn't passing with how nothing changes. He's one of the few actively trying to find a way out, but I think he's just soul searching. "It'll take more than a lifetime to finish all the books here," I reply. "When I'm done, I'll consider taking up another activity, like devising escape methods."

Without day or night, the library is always lit the same way: a grayish orange from the sad excuse of a sunset we're not sure is actually the sun, more a hole poked through infinite space, lending a ray of light—although if it were a hole, we might've been able to trace our way out. I like to lay curled up behind the Y through Z bookshelves where the books seem least touched, carpet most unworn, lightbulbs most dusty. There's a small, Alice-in-Wonderland-sized square door along the wall that once led to storage and laptop carts, but now opens to a void lit by sporadic supernova-like blasts I'm convinced are the manifestations of highly magnetic neutron stars. I've crawled through the door several times before, trying to reach out towards the cosmic bursts like they're puffs of cotton, but I've never touched anything solid and gave up. I doubt exploding stars are a means of escape anyway.

We all get food at noon in the cafeteria because no one wants to man the stations the entire day. We take turns being on meal prep duty based on a daily rotation schedule established by the 'natural leaders' of the group, which includes Junlan. These were the kids who volunteered to organize chocolate-covered-pretzel and bubble tea fundraisers, led their sports teams at away meets, speak naturally at a volume louder than most of us. They call themselves The Council. We've figured out how to pry open the vending machines and gorge ourselves on flaming hot Funyuns, although we got sick of them fast, especially after they self-restocked and we'd gone days eating only unnaturally bright red foods. I tell Junlan I miss the beef tripe soup Ma used to make, especially dipping the organ meats in hot oil and the daikon in crystal sugar. Junlan says there are bigger things to worry about.

Junlan and the other Council members decide to implement The Strategy, in which groups of us must go on expeditions and report back our observations. They're big on the scientific method and think we can hypothesize ourselves out of here.

When we still shared a bedroom and dad used the spare bedroom as a study, Junlan told me I'd grow taller by hanging myself upside down, a statistically proven method according to him, and I'd hang with my legs bent over the stair railing, blood rushing to my head, eyes closed so I wouldn't realize when the stars filled my vision, as Junlan timed me. He told me it was working despite our lack of a control. "Of course it's effective," he said. "Gravity is squeezing your cartilage all day, every day. It's only natural to stretch yourself back out." Junlan doesn't want me to be short like Ma or Waipo—dwarf-like women who make up for their height with their ability to out-argue anyone, a feat made possible by their unwavering belief in their correctness and their classic condescending grimaces that make them look twenty years older: the snake-raising, poison-feeding witch age rather than naive Asian lady age. I'm not like them though: Junlan says I shut down and evaporate when the old grandpa who mans a small stand by the entrance of the Da Zhong Hua grocery store asks if I want a free mechanical pencil or a can of cold oolong tea.

In what Junlan calls the pilot of The Strategy, the first assigned group jumps off the edge of our plane into the void. They disappear instantly into the dark: one moment we hear them shouting goodbye and we're replying with good luck, the next moment, it's silent besides the twins' Andy and Allen's asthmatic wheezing. We return to the school building, quiet and solemn like we've sent them to their deaths even though, I'm certain, no one can die here. The Council christens them as 'Adventurers' and decides to call all future groups 'Adventurers' instead of sacrifices. I don't say anything though because Ma has always taught me 'mute eats dumplings, heart inside keeps count', my botched translation which Junlan finds hysterical, but he hasn't proposed an alternative and it doesn't sound as cool to say 'you should clearly understand the situation but shut up about it'. The first group of Adventurers reappears the next day exactly where they stood before stepping off the plane, like newly stacked chess pieces, unworn and unused. They say they don't remember where they went, and by the time they became aware, they had returned.

"You can't keep kicking people off the edge," I tell Junlan in the library when he visits me behind the bookshelves. My back is against the shelves, knees curled toward my chest, and he's sitting with his arms hooked around his legs like he's trying to make himself appear smaller for once.

"What else are we supposed to do?" Junlan asks.

He's not looking for an answer. He's looking for some kind of enlightenment, the type of revelation Ma described as earth-shattering when she suddenly decided to pack our bags and move us across the country to a house situated near a creek the real estate agent claimed once housed bright red coho salmon, a species now nearly extinct besides the few who manage to maneuver through the culverts under roads and complete their migration. Ma took all the gold jewelry which she bought for our future weddings, and left dad with the tarnished silver bangle which she said incorporated his soul and spiritual essence—in other words, not much, she said. Dad was only good for money, and you didn't need to live with someone for money unless it purchased emotional support, but emotional support held zero fiscal value in Ma's eyes because if you couldn't eat it or directly use it to purchase something edible, it was useless. They're still married on paper, and dad continues to get his biweekly paychecks deposited into the shared Wells Fargo account, likely because he's too lazy to dig up his personal bank account's routing number. Ma rubs Junlan the wrong way though, maybe because she once forgot him at one of those after school prep programs and he was stuck listening to some redhead prattling on about her Tamagotchis and Webkinz for hours, so he didn't listen when she told us 'dreams and romance are for people who didn't eat enough rice growing up, you can do much better'.

"Chill?" I suggest, scratching a stray piece of skin from the corner of my fingernail, wincing as I pick it off.

"Something's bound to change if we observe long enough," Junlan murmurs. "You know, like how you have to watch animals for hours before they'll do something interesting." He nods to himself, straightens his back and stands, his joints seemingly reinvigorated with a sense of purpose.

When I was little and believed Disney princesses were an occupation, I thought Junlan was a hero with a neverending list of savior requests, and he'd prioritize me: fend off unwanted attention in the sketchy parts of the neighborhood, walk me home when I was out late for extracurriculars, bring me my lunch money when I forgot it on the kitchen table. He's everyone's savior now—tells them when to eat, when to clean, how to spend their time in this timeless purgatory, what to do when they're homesick. I can see Junlan running for president if we ever get back because if he can turn a group of adolescents into functional, productive citizens, he can save the world if it needs saving.

The second batch of Adventurers experiment with destruction. Junlan marks off the weight room at the corner of the school and tells us to stay far from the yellow tape. We watch as the Adventurers begin to dent the walls, drop weights onto the ground, crash dumbbells into mirrors, stab poles into windows. To no one's surprise, the wreck and damage vanish the next day, so they set fire to the yoga mats and treadmills, and we watch from afar: the smoke floating upward in great, monolithic clouds eventually fading out—the gray plumes, the burning scent, the sharp sting—eaten by the void. The yoga mats, once ashes, are rolled up neatly in the gym, vinyl sheets of bright turquoise stacked on orange stacked on magenta. We sniff. No one can detect the coppery, metallic, tar-like scent anymore. The matches used to start the fire are back in the matchbox, the heads red and unoxidized, the phosphorous black strip unscratched. "This place is self-correcting," I tell Junlan. "Like a cactus. I think we're better off keeping to ourselves." Which is exactly what I do, what Ma does, what dad does, what Junlan seems incapable of because he's got an inability to sit still at best, a hero-complex at worst.

I discover a stack of unused construction paper and printer paper in the library office and decide to take up paper cutting. It takes more time than I anticipate because I first need to learn to draw, and only then can I carve out my lines of wheat stems and imperfect moons and curled petals and pied magpies. I learn to draw fast, ignoring the details I can leave up to my brain to fill. What

I don't finish in a day reverts to blank paper the next. Junlan thinks I've always been good at these sorts of arts and crafts: seeing ordinary objects in negative space, composing bodies into abstract forms, handling tools with flexibility and precision, but it boils down to practice and a distraction-free environment, easily obtained when your only friend is the home ed teacher who finds you interesting because you know how to use rice flour. It's repetition disguised as talent. Ma says not to be ashamed because hard workers end up far more successful than any prodigy—just look at cousin Justin who was a world-class violinist at five and recently fled back to Beijing after his girlfriend called the police on him for holding her hostage, and now he's mooching off his parents' money which doesn't seem like a terrible outcome for Justin to me. I was born in the year of the ox which Ma says is her biggest regret, not that she could've helped when she gave birth although she insists if only she'd found her fermented miso chocolate bars sooner, my delivery wouldn't have been pushed out of the year of the rat. "It's not your fault," she reassured me when I ranked second in the Chinese handwriting competition. "The ox was too stupid and got deceived by the mouse. You can't change how you're born." But I'm thinking, maybe the ox didn't care so much about the mouse riding on its head; they were both heading in the same direction and as long as they arrived, did order matter?

I'm part of the third batch of Adventurers. Junlan tried to get me out of it because he thinks I can't handle risk-taking behavior, but the others insisted he was being biased. Our task is to bring some samples of material from outside our plane.

"How are we supposed to do that when the previous groups weren't even able to remember their time outside this area?" the others in my group ask.

"I don't know, you figure it out," the Council answers.

We stand by the edge of the plane, peering down into the dark, reaching our arms out attempting to grab onto anything solid.

"Do they expect us to do this all day?" one person in my group asks. The rest of us mumble our agreement and stop, deciding to sit and wait out our scheduled 'work' time. I retreat to the library and pry open the square door. This is where I go when I don't want anyone—even Junlan—to find me. I wonder what it'd feel like to cup a stellar explosion within my hands, if there'd be dust revolving around the light, if it'd glow hot like iron, if they'd continue to pulsate like lighthouse beams guiding lost ships home. I crawl in and grasp for a ripple of light. I feel something slip between my fingers—faint, almost non-existent, like a thread of silk I've pulled and pulled from Ma's qipao she wore during her wedding reception, after cursing and stripping off the white A-Liner. I clench my fist quickly, hoping to grab onto something, but it disappears as soon as my fingernails dig into my palms. I try again, leaning forward on my hands and knees, closer and closer until my outstretched palm can entirely cover the light. You've got to have good reflexes to catch entities, that dislike being observed, by surprise. Ma could snatch grasshoppers with her chopsticks, crush their midsections instantly between worn bamboo and flick their guts into the grass before plucking more, insisting the grasshoppers had ravaged the garden she regularly forgot to water and prune. She tried to teach us how to wield chopsticks like weapons with marshmallows first, then fish eyeballs, ice cubes, and finally marbles which were the hardest to balance despite Junlan's ability to pick them up instantly, gracefully like he'd been born for crafts, a talent Ma claimed went wasted since he was too preoccupied with social networking. It took me a day to accomplish what Junlan could figure out in thirty minutes: jabbing ice cubes from one bowl to another without dropping a single one, writing our names the elegant way with a mao bi, embroidering the panda pattern Ma bought us to decorate our hand towels, copying and shading the basket of lychee and guavas with one HB pencil and an eraser.

I exhale, close my eyes. I've got to be patient. Things don't fall into my hands like they seem to do with Junlan's. Ma believes there's a certain beauty in trying so hard you'd rather fail fast than keep struggling and make stupid mistakes. Sometimes she cites dad as a stupid mistake, but other times she says she's a genius for snagging a steady supply of supplementary income.

When I feel the slightest breeze, no more than a memory of a ghost, I swipe my arm and close my fist. There's something between my fingers beating weakly, even softer than my pulse, and I stare at my grip, wondering if it'll escape as soon as I loosen a single finger. I loosen my index finger and thumb anyway. The beating stops, and I gradually peel my other fingers away too. A butterfly sits in my hand, its wings glowing and dimming, shimmering like fireworks, occasionally disseminating light over my palm even though I know light isn't solid. It's got to be some other type of matter, one we've never seen before in the real world. I cover the butterfly with another hand, cupping it to my chest as though my back is a fortress. I get the feeling it won't revive the same way we do and I've got to preserve its life here, untouched and undissected, flickering off in its own universe. I'm ok with not knowing if it's capable of dying, how it came from a library closet, if it can pollinate flowers. I tell Junlan all the time I'm not dumb, just selectively curious, with a different ranking of priorities. He's too hung up on returning to the real world, where he still has adults to kiss up to and peers to mentor. "He'll go far as I did," Ma had told me while we folded paper cranes, but I thought he was already so far away. "I ditched it all in the end, too much effort spending thirty minutes every morning to put on makeup."

When we meet back to report our findings, I stay quiet as we're lectured for not trying hard enough.

"At least the previous groups took some sort of action. You can't just sit around and expect us to consider this a contribution," the Council lectures.

The girl next to me, who spent the time we were supposed to be gathering samples filing her nails and playing sudoku on her phone, snorts just loud enough so I can hear. At the sound, Junlan glares in our direction.

"We have better things to do," the girl says.

"Like playing sudoku?" Junlan asks.

"It's a game I can win. What do I get out of trying to grab a handful of infinite space?" she shoots back.

I shut my eyes, pretending whoever I can't see also can't see me. Junlan calls it turtling, caging myself into a dark shell, a blanket of bone and keratin, a universe I've conjured from my will or fear or tenacity, unbreakable by reality. I suspect, if I open my eyes and make contact with Junlan, he'll be able to tell I'm hiding something, and then he'll cajole it out of me because he knows I'm easily guilted by his 'you're doing it for all of us' arguments, and then I'll lead him and his band of world-saviors to the square door, point to the dark, the fireworks of light, the trail of a butterfly whom they'll say isn't a butterfly but a specimen, a sample, the key to our escape and take it with them to the chemistry lab where they'll rip specks of a wing with forceps, attempt to align it with our universe, then wake up the next day expecting a fully regenerated, intact butterfly to be shimmering on the table only for it to be long gone, for us to be back in real-world class, for me to wander to the bathroom, winding around every classroom until I've reached the sink and gently, like a finch, vomit. Junlan said the vomiting problem would go away if I focused more on school, less on nebulous things like how Nüwa patched the holes in heaven and molded humans to cure her loneliness—she should've just built a world without loneliness instead.

I haven't vomited since winding up here, although Junlan hasn't realized.

© 2022 Lucy Zhang

Science Fantasy - 3230 words

About the Author

Lucy Zhang writes, codes and watches anime. Her work has appeared in *AAWW*, *SmokeLong Quarterly*, *Passages North*, and elsewhere. Her chapbook *HOLLOWED* is forthcoming from Thirty West Publishing, and her micro-chapbook *ABSORPTION* is forthcoming from Harbor Review in 2022. Find her at https://kowaretasekai.wordpress.com/ or on Twitter **@Dango_Ramen**.

Sine The End

Claire McNerney

The modern pop song structure goes as follows: intro, verse, chorus, verse, chorus, bridge, chorus, out.

— INTRO —

We were eighteen and full of ourselves when we decided to start a band. Phoebe could play the keyboard, Seb had a vintage drumset, and I had bought a shiny electric guitar with my graduation money. We met twice a week to practice together in Seb's garage with the door open so that all the neighbors could hear, but I wrote more often than that in my bedroom, alone, with a headphone in one ear.

In the sunlit suburbs before the Deaths, things weren't bad. But 'bad' is exactly how I made them out to be. I thought that niceness was stupid, that things had to be angsty to be good. So the smooth roads turned into cracked asphalt, the nice little houses into derelict prisons of our lives. I went so far as to curse the sun for its brightness.

When the Hot Topic at the mall shut down, I wrote about the end of the world. There was barely any metaphor beneath all that violence. Phoebe added some minor harmonies and suggested I add imagery inspired by the far away drought and war-torn countries.

— VERSE —

Phoebe's dead now. And those far away countries probably don't look too different from here. I wouldn't know, TVs don't work anymore so there's no news from that far away. It's bad here, I'll tell you that much. It's been bad since the first Death, the one that took Phoebe.

She died far from home. We said we were on tour, but really we had just driven three hours north to the only venue that would let us play. We pretended to be pissed that they weren't even going to pay us, but really, we were ecstatic to perform. We set up the stage, squeaked out a mic check, and headed backstage to prepare. It was there, in the molding green room of a concert venue that was more bar than floor, that the first Death hit us.

It wasn't a disease, though it killed the same. It was more like gas, like fog. Seb opened the door for a smoke and it came flooding in, too opaque to be air, too thin to be water. Phoebe choked and coughed on the gas for what felt like forever. Then she stopped, and I immediately wished she would start choking again. Then, at least, she'd be alive.

I didn't dare open my mouth while Phoebe sputtered in the gas. After an agonizing hour, once Seb and I realized we could safely breathe in it, I wished I had. Maybe it would have been easier if I said goodbye.

The first Death lasted for eleven months. Almost a year. We learned to live without the sun I had once pretended to hate, and we pretended to know how to live without the people it had killed. Ten percent of the population, according to the papers (there were still papers back then, before the other Deaths, before those of us unlucky enough to survive started to tear each other apart). But if Phoebe was the only one who had died, it would have felt the same to me.

We brought her body back with us, but her parents had also died in that first Death, so Seb and I were the ones to bury her. At her funeral, I played one of the songs we once wrote together. Maybe it was tasteless, but I chose the one about that other end of the world. It had always been her favorite.

— CHORUS —

I still dye my hair with stockpiled drugstore bottles, even though they don't work that well anymore. I've got a dozen in my backpack, all pulled out of their boxes to save space. I burn the instructions for tinder—I've got the procedure memorized. When I joined my current traveling group, dye was my go-to pick-up thing. Everyone has one, something to pick up at a big-box store or convenience store. Something light and easy to carry. My groupmates carry earrings and My Little Ponies and Kinder Eggs long-gone-stale. I chose dye.

It's funny because I used to be so strict on only doing black, but I've done loads of colors now. I've been blonde and green and blue and five million shades of red. Today, though, I have black. It's the closest thing I've got to a treat. Looking at my crunchy dyed hair reminds me of the life I used to live, with all those purposefully ripped jeans and monochrome outfits.

We're between towns, stopped off the road in a gas station long since raided. Dinner is Kiki's deer jerky, and a couple of late summer berries Peter found in the forest. They're all ten years younger than me and far better survivors. I'm dead weight in this group, but they keep me around. I sing them songs, tell them stories about how things used to be when there was electricity, and describe old movies and TV. They give me food and protection. It's not a fair trade, but hey! I'm not going to tell them that.

Tonight's light chatter is guessing about the next Death. It shouldn't be funny, with all those who've died, but it somehow is.

"A plague of kittens," someone says.

"The roads turn into water."

"All the trees come alive," says Edna.

"The trees are already alive," I reply.

"You know what I mean."

I do. Between the seemingly dead trees, the stars shine brighter than they ever did. I pray to every tiny star that there is not a 'next Death', but it's only a matter of time. It always was.

— VERSE —

Seb and I stuck together after Phoebe died, and we made it through a fair share of Deaths. Rabid animals, drought, locusts (believe it or not). There weren't many people left. We had both lost our families, and nothing was keeping us in our falling-apart homes with their useless appliances. By the time we made our way out into the countryside, the suburbs were ablaze with violence. Somehow, we managed to escape it, with our cart full of raided groceries and the open road before us. We started, well, not dating, but the post-apocalyptic equivalent of it. We were all we had.

We found an abandoned farm. The house was in good shape, and it was nice to sleep on a mattress instead of just camping equipment. We cleared the fields out and planted some seeds from the barn. Somehow, they managed to sprout. It was spring, and the orchards were abloom in pink and white. At night, we drank cider from the farmhouse cellar. He played drums on turned-over pots around the fire as I strummed my old acoustic guitar. For the first time, I thought we could have a life again.

But just when it looked like things were going to be okay, Seb died. He cut his leg trying to move the rusty old tractor out of the field. His leg started to swell, but all the medicine in the old farmhouse's cabinets was expired. I didn't want to leave him alone, but I risked riding a bike to the nearest drugstore, to try and find something— anything—that could save him, but there were no more antibiotics. We tried the expired stuff anyways. It didn't work. Seb made it through so much, so many Deaths. But it didn't matter how strong he was. A small cut in the leg was enough to kill him.

I buried him near the farmhouse with his drumsticks crossed over his chest. I tried to get on with my life, to tend to the farm, but every time I knelt by the newly sprouted plants, I was reminded of Seb. I was heartbroken. I let the weeds in.

Three weeks later, a new Death of wind tore the farm apart, and the house with it. Safe in the basement, I drank until the cider was gone, and then I left, too.

— CHORUS —

We're camping out at a settlement for the week, a former Y camp Kiki went to as a kid. The wooden buildings remind me too much of the farmhouse, and I spend the afternoon anxiously gathering firewood. Addie, who was born after the Deaths started, tells me that she likes it here as we chop the dried logs. She wants to stay forever.

We never stay.

Still, around tonight's campfire (roaring in a big stone fire pit), I try to play cheery songs very unlike my old sad ones. These kids don't need to hear about teen angst they'll never get to experience and drugs that aren't around anymore. They get enough sorrow in their everyday lives, I don't need to add to it.

Midway through the evening, I run out of camp songs to sing and have to switch back to oldies and pop-rock. I never learned very many camp songs. I was a girl scout in elementary school, but I stopped in middle school after I got my double piercings. The leader said I couldn't wear them to camp, so I quit in protest. I was always protesting something, but never anything that mattered. I wish I would have taken my doubles out for that weekend if just so I could better remember the tunes of the songs.

Edna announced that she set up rabbit traps in the woods, which means we're going to have to stay here a bit longer to clean and cook the meat. Usually, I would protest staying in one place for too long—it's dangerous. But this far in the mountains, we're decently safe. Maybe the wait won't be so bad this time. There's a blackberry bramble behind the cabin I'm sleeping in. Some of the berries will ripen while we're here. That's worth waiting for, I think.

— BRIDGE —

I won't regret the songs I wrote, no matter how my memories of them make me feel. It's like there's a hole where my heart used to be and every time I sing one of my old songs, it grows a little wider.

That sounds so angsty. Twenty years ago I would have used a line like that to describe my anger at the student body's general lack of thick eyeliner. I can hear myself whining about nobody liking me. That was never true.

But it isn't nostalgia or embarrassment that makes it hard to listen to my old songs. It's that my lines about the end of the world now feel like premonitions, or worse: like summoning spells. Like I sang all this misery into existence.

I know that's ridiculously untrue. No one's that powerful, and the Deaths aren't anything like my song lyrics. But some days it still feels like it's all my fault.

— CHORUS —

A fire burned down one of the cabins last night. We hauled buckets from the lake in the dark, the twelve of us working together better than we ever have. We put the fire out, though the sun was nearly up by the time the embers stopped smoldering. We got lucky. It wasn't a Death. The fire didn't hurt anything except for Pats' bedroll. We'll have to get her a spare next time we go through a town.

I let her stay in my cabin. I usually sleep alone, but Pats is eighteen and old enough to not be a nuisance to anyone but herself. Her bunkmates blamed her for starting the fire and refuse to let her into their new cabin. She was trying to smoke some pine needles. Stupid, yes, but not a crime. She'll learn. And if they won't forgive her, I won't let them listen to me play guitar. It's too harsh a world to hold a grudge.

Under the warm afternoon sun, I tie my old fishing line to a stick and try to fish in the lake. I only catch two, but that's enough for a bit of a meal. As I clean them, I listen to Kiki and Dev talk about building a vegetable garden where the old cabin was. Something about the remains of fires being good fertilizer for crops. Peter says he found some seeds in one of the sheds. He doesn't know if they're any good, but he's willing to try.

We voted at dinner, and nearly everyone agreed. We're staying here, at least for a bit. I suppose Addie got her wish. And this place is nice. It's so far from any dangerous towns, we don't need to worry about people. Just nature, I suppose, and Deaths.

I mix some blackberries in with boiled water and call it wine. We deserve a celebration.

— OUT —

At sixty, I'm dying, hair naturally gray. It's shockingly peaceful for a disease. The Deaths keep coming, but so do the lives. Every year, we have to build a new cabin for our growing town. We keep farming and manage to breed some livestock. People get married, and I play at their weddings. More people die, and I play at their funerals. I play until I can't anymore, and then I teach the children how to play. Teenagers in this new world are faced with more hardships than I could have ever known at their age, but they find ways to create light. One girl, inspired, carves a wooden drumset. A boy figures out how to make guitar strings from entrails, the way they used to be made. They are filled with so much joy, playing together.

I have lived longer than anyone I know. I see so much pain that it becomes a part of me. But then there are moments of music, moments of light, moments that remind me not of the past but the future, and I am glad. They'll play such beautiful music at my funeral.

Fantasy - 2329 words

About the Author

Claire McNerney is an actor, student, and writer from California, where she currently attends UCSD. She enjoys, among other things, floral ice cream flavors. Follow her on Twitter **@claire_mcnerney** or Instagram **@o.h.c.l.a.i.r.e** to say hello and see what she does next!

Adjectives of Annihilation

B. Morris Allen

My parents could never describe it. The ravages of an increasingly stratified world, of bitter philosophical division, of a climate run amok. The devastation of war. The nightmare of departure.

"Nothing survived," said my poet father.

"Probably nothing survived," amended my mother, who'd been a particle physicist, and more comfortable with uncertainty.

They were farmers now. We were all farmers. "Wheat feet," my father called us. They said he'd been a noted poet, back on Earth. Here on Doilea, he was a reluctantly competent miller.

"There's nothing to go back to, in any case," he said. They agreed on that. "Our life is here. Life is here." And on that too, since we'd only ever reached one other planet capable of sustaining us. One isolated community, one rickety ship, one newly invented stasis generator, one desperate gamble. One halfway Terran planet covered in water, algae, and some lumps of rock. Atmosphere, oxygen, a cold orange sun, and a place to set down. That was the only choice we'd had, and we'd taken it gladly.

"How's the crushing going?" my mother asked as if particle physics made her an expert on rock dust.

"Fine, I guess," I said. My mind was still on Rodica, and her crazy plan to refit the shuttle, get up to the Calator, and go back to see what was left of Earth.

"Grinding," my father said. "They're grinding the rock, not crushing it."

My mother waved away the distinction as inconsequential. "Either way."

"You wouldn't want us crushing the grain," he pointed out. "We'd have wheat paste rather than flour." He was a man of details, which made him a good miller. 'Poetry is about precision,' he liked to say. 'Not accuracy,' my mother would always add, and they would laugh.

"It's fine," I said before they could get sidetracked by semantics. "We're...Sorin has a new idea for mixing different grades of dust with sewage and seawater, and then leaching out the salt." Doilea's seas were relatively low in salinity, which made our lives easier. "It should be more...soil-like." 'Dirty' was what Sorin called it, but I couldn't say that with a poet across the table. "We should have enough for that new beet field in a week or so." Why anyone would want more beets was a mystery to me, but that's what we'd brought. I blamed Moldova, the little country we'd left behind, just before there stopped being countries.

"Hear that, Oana?" my father asked with a smirk? "Three sentences in a row, and not one about Earth! I think our Crinitsa's sullen, resentful period may finally be ending." He winked at me to take the sting out.

"I'll believe it when I see it," Mom said as if he hadn't just underlined the evidence. I rolled my eyes to make her happy, and the conversation went back to farming, as every conversation on Doilea eventually did.

————

"There's nothing there," Ilya said, ever the cynic. But he still hung out with us and did his part to help with the shuttle every evening in the hour between study and sleep.

"There might be," said Rodica. "You've heard them talk," meaning our elders. "Something might have survived. There could be...lizards!" We shared a moment of silence to wonder at those colorful, self-armored creatures of myth. One more thing we hadn't brought with us in our headlong flight.

"I don't have to listen to the old folk," insisted Ilya. "I was there. We all were." We'd been infants, mostly, but technically he was right.

"You were four," I pointed out. "Pass me that multimeter. You don't really remember anything."

"I remember enough." By which he meant he knew it had been frightening; enough so that even the weird freefall of the ship had been preferable.

"It's been a long time," said Rodica, wedging a circuit board into place with a violence that made me wince. She was better with ideas and plumbing, and I raised an eyebrow to Ilya so that he quietly edged her out of her place by the control panel. "OK, maybe no lizards. But there could be algae growing." That was her favorite theory. "Maybe someone eating the algae."

"You want algae? We got algae!" That was Miruna, who'd been doing something I didn't understand with the thrusters. "Algae for lunch, algae for dinner. Next up, algae for breakfast."

"Bread," Ilya said, his voice muffled by gauges, wires, and plastic. "It's bread we want."

"Working on it," said Miruna, whose day job was coaxing limited quantities of yeast into a sustainable, harvestable colony. "If they'd only started earlier, instead of leaving it until a decade in—"

"Now I know it's time to turn in," interrupted Rodica. "If I have to hear Miruna complain about saccharomyces staging one more time, I'm heading for orbit now, if I have to jump."

"Look, it's just a fact. If they had just set aside some of the yeast we brought, instead of wasting it—"

"On food," Ilya muttered, as he slid out from under the half-restored control panel.

"—we wouldn't have had to culture it from—"

"Please don't say it," said Rodica, clambering out of the cockpit to the echoing space that had once been a passenger compartment.

"—humans," Miruna finished with a smug smirk.

There was a collective "Ugh!", and we all slid down the ladder and off to our respective beds.

———

"Stop! Stop!" There was a hammering on the side of my little cabin, and I tripped the toggle that turned off the grinder—an improvised mechanism of augers, drills, and scrap metal sides that did a surprisingly good job of converting Doilean stone to arable soil base.

"What's up?" I called. I took out my earplugs—precious shreds of cotton wool—and slid aside the sheet of plastic that kept some of the dust away from jury-rigged controls.

Ms. Codru was staring at a jagged sliver of steel, long and thin, with regular threads along one side. One of the drill bits.

"It's broken," she said dully. "We're all broken. No dust, no soil, no crops. No beets," she said as if beets were the key to our survival.

"I...I'm sorry," I stammered. How had I not noticed? Had there been no change in the sound, the rhythm, the shuddering feel of my little perch in the control cabin?

"Sorry. Sorry! Do you think 'sorry' will fix this, girl? Do you think 'sorry' will grow beans and nuts and apples? Do you think—"

"I'm sorry," I pleaded. And I was. This was a disaster. We had other bits, of course, but with fewer bits, the grinding would take longer, they'd be more stressed, and then more would break. We'd have no more soil, no more fields, and we have to stick with hydroponics, and we didn't have the material for more vats, so we'd probably keep eating algae, and—

"Take your sorry and go home. Dream about Earth on your own time, you stupid girl. Dream about Earth, since there's no earth here. Not now; not anymore. Go!" She gripped the broken drill bit as if she wanted to stab it through my heart, and I ran.

I was still sitting in our living/kitchen when my mother came home.

"I'm sorry," I said before she could do more than raise an eyebrow. "I'm so sorry." I threw my arms around her from my chair and cried the whole story into her belly like a child.

"So let me get this straight," she said after we'd disentangled at last and the tears had started to dry. "The drill broke."

"The bit broke. And—"

"And so now we have fewer drill bits."

"We don't have soil. And that means no food—"

"And that means your dramatic days aren't quite over yet, poet's daughter. Not quite." She laid a hand on my arm as I pulled back, stung. She laughed, and anger rose in my chest, pushing out the guilt. "Do you think that our survival hinges on one drill bit? That we aren't clever enough to find another way out? Don't be foolish, Crina. Don't prove that woman right." Her jaw set. "And as for Iulia Codru…"

There was a scrape of footsteps on the stones outside, and I looked out.

"Oh, no." My angry courage fled again, leaving my heart a wasteland of sick certainty. "It's her. And Dad." I could see them coming down the path, Ms. Codru's face stony, my father's wrinkled in concern.

"I'll deal with this." I could see the anger and determination in my mother's eyes and took what comfort I could. Stupid and foolish I might be, but not alone. She stood and threw the door open.

"Don't say it, Oana," came Ms. Codru's voice. "You're right. I'm here to apologize."

My mother closed her mouth. "You'd better be," I heard her hiss as she stepped aside.

"Crina," said Ms. Codru from just inside the door. I wiped my face, sure that there were still trails of snot and tears to give me away. "I'm sorry. I was angry, and I misspoke. I was wrong. You couldn't have known, not from that tiny little cabin, with all that noise. I just…I was so looking forward to them, you know. The beets." She smiled a tense little smile. "I shouldn't have taken it out on you."

I wanted to say something sharp, angry, precise. To take out on her the misery I still felt, the guilt I still carried, the certainty I'd always be the girl who broke the drill, who threw away the earth. But I couldn't.

"What is it with you all and beets?" I asked instead. And to my surprise, she laughed. And cried. We both did, and even my mother's angry face softened a little.

My father slid past the women. "My little poet," he said, and kissed me on the head, even though I hadn't said anything that rhymed or evoked an image or used stiff, pretentious language.

————

There were consequences, of course. Not for me. I kept working the grinder, alert to every shake, every grumble, every buzz that might indicate a problem. I took out the earplugs for a while, until Ms. Codru noticed that I couldn't hear anything at the end of the shift, and then my father chastised me and started coming by unexpectedly to make sure I had them in. I knew that meant the mill was either closed or in the hands of his assistant Stela, and I knew how he felt about that. So I put them back in, and life went back to normal.

Except that we had a community meeting to talk about it. Ms. Codru said the bit was broken, and there were no replacements. And then Sorin, who was not much older than me, but had emerged as our lead soil chemist, talked about how we had to have finer soil than the gravel we could get from crushing, and how microbes from our sewage would take too long to break it down, because they weren't lithophages, which I wasn't sure was even a thing. Then my father suggested we could use a grindstone like in the mill, but it had taken a long time to make that one. And then Andrei said he could rig a mechanical water hammer, which seemed to be a way of using gravel in a waterfall to break itself down, but he would need fine filters, and we didn't have any. It went on for hours until someone pointed out that the shuttle had a fine mesh lining sealing the bulkheads.

That was when Rodica stepped in. "We can't use the shuttle lining," she said as if it were a truth not to be gainsaid. There was a flood of gainsaying, but she stood her ground. "The shuttle is our way back to the Calator," she insisted. "And the Calator is our way back to Earth."

There was argument, but in the end, the adults agreed—there was nothing to go back to on Earth.

"Anyway, there's no point," said my mother. "It took us a hundred years in stasis to get here. It would take a hundred years to get back. And a hundred years again to come home. Who would do that?" I could see the tension in her neck as she sat beside me, and I knew what she meant. 'Why would my daughter leave me?'

I hadn't thought it through until that moment. I'd focused on the adventure, on Rodica's stories of magical, color-changing chameleons, of the weird and wonderful species a resurgent Earth would have developed in the stew of heat and radiation man had left behind. I'd known we'd have to go into stasis, of course. I knew more about the stasis generator than anyone but half-crazy Mr. Morar who'd invented it. I'd just never thought about what it meant.

"Some people would," said Rodica, who'd never gotten along with her father, and whose mother had stayed behind on Earth.

They argued more, and the tide was strong against Rodica and for cannibalizing the shuttle.

"We can replace the lining," said someone. "Someday."

"Someday," retorted Rodica. "It will take decades before we can manufacture lining like that. Maybe forever, if we all turn into farmers, and only farmers. We're better than that. We're space travelers!"

She was losing, though, and we could all see it. Immediate survival will always win out over dreams, with most people. That's why we're still here.

But what's life for, without dreams? "There's another way," I said at last, as momentum gathered for a vote. "We can finish the shuttle, and use it to go back to the Calator."

Eyebrows raised, and a murmur went around the crowd. Rodica looked at me hopefully, and I could see the hunger in her eyes, and the dream still burning.

"I thought of that," Andrei said immediately. "The lining of the Calator is entirely different. And there's no other fabric up there. We stripped that thing pretty thoroughly."

"No, not for a filter." I swallowed and forced myself to look at Rodica. "The stasis generator uses large worm screws. We could use those as drill bits." Rodica's face sagged, and I watched as the light in her eyes began to fade. "They wouldn't last as long, but there are half a dozen of them. We could use the shuttle to go get them." And kill Rodica's hope of getting to Earth any time soon.

The decision was unanimous, with the exception of Rodica, who stood broken as the rest knit together in planning for a future, and who stalked away before they even got around to voting.

————

"Go away."

"No, listen."

"Go away!" Rodica kicked a leg out toward me as she struggled with a rheostat she was installing the wrong way around.

"It's better this way," I said.

"Better!" She gave up on the rheostat—part of the shuttle's attitude control system—and turned on me. I was glad to see the fire in her eyes, even if it was only anger. "You trapped us here, you…you traitor, you bitch, you farmer. Without the stasis generator, we can't go back. We can't see what's happened, whether…"

"Whether anyone's alive." And I knew now that that was what it was about, what it had always been about, for her. "It's been a hundred years, Roda. More. She's gone. She's always been gone."

"Maybe." Reluctant, still angry, but without an argument to turn to.

"We can still go, Roda. Someday."

"Someday," she spat. "You and your somedays." She waved a hand to include me and the rest of the colony in this blind 'you'.

"Worm screws are easier to make than hull lining. In a decade, maybe, we could make something that would work. Maybe do without them entirely. I've got some ideas. The screws are used to adjust the focus plates, but we could do that a different way. We know more about stasis now than when Morar built the generator. Then it was just an idea—a proof of concept. Now, we've used it; we know it works. We don't need the screws at all. I mean, we need something, but it doesn't have to be screws."

"How long?" She was still angry, still bitter. But still friends, I thought.

"I don't know. Five years? Ten? A while."

"Oh. But you can do it?" Dreams need so little to grow on; just enough to sink in a few tenacious roots, and they'll survive, somehow.

"I can do it." I smiled. "We can do it." But I knew, already, that I would not be going. Not in five years, or ten. Not until we were safe here, until my father and mother were old, until one broken machine couldn't bring us to the brink of crisis. But if making the stasis generator work was what Roda wanted, I would do it.

————

"Your father's a scientist," my mother said, sliding a lopsided, slightly burned piece of bread onto my plate. "He and your friend Miruna with her yeast."

"I'm a miller," he protested from where he stood by the hotplate, heating algae for porridge.

"Being a scientist isn't hard," she said. "If you know the difference between precision and accuracy, you're a scientist. And if you can grind wheat fine enough to bake bread."

"Your mother's a poet," my father said. "Which means she knows what's important."

"And that's bread?" I asked, fulfilling my quotient of teenage cynicism for the day.

"It's beauty," he said, kissing her on the back of the neck.

"And truth," she said, rolling her eyes and sitting down to eat.

"I'm going to throw up," I said, going a little over my quotient for luck.

"How's the shuttle?" my father asked, sliding a bowl of algal goop in front of me. I laid the bread on top to cover it up.

"Almost ready. We can go up any time, really. It's just the automatic docking mount that needs adjusting."

"And the stasis generator?" My mother's voice was calm, but I could feel the tension in her from across the table.

"I have a plan." It was a good one, too, needing just a few careful measurements and a set of limited actuators to correct for heat expansion. It would work.

"Oh." The word conveyed far more than she'd said. "Rodica will be happy."

I laid a hand on hers, comforting her for once. "She's happy now, I think." We both were. We'd grown closer over the last months, fixing the shuttle. Last night, I'd thought for a minute that she was about to kiss me, or I her, before Ilya came in and interrupted us. Rodica talked less now about the trip to Earth, and more about the shuttle, and about her day job in the hydroponics section. "Have you seen her transplants in the new field?"

"Like the ears of tiny green rabbits," my father said, "just about to poke their curious heads up out of the soil."

"Native Doileans," I said. "Like the rest of us."

"Beets Earth any day," my mother said. We stared at her. "Get it? Beets, like the seedlings."

I threw my bread at her, algae streaked as it was. My father just shuddered. But she was right; it did beat Earth. This was home now; the only home we had. Hard and poor and limited, but clean and fresh and just starting to be green. Maybe Earth was greening too; maybe it was recovering from what we'd done to it, maybe something still lived there. We'd find out someday, but until then, it could get along just as well without us, and in the interim, maybe we'd learn to love a planet—to take just a part of

Doilea and make it ours, and leave the rest to native algae and rock and sea. Maybe I'd learn to love beets. Everything's possible, if you let your dreams grow big enough.

Science Fiction - 3331 words

About the Author

B. Morris Allen is a biochemist turned activist turned lawyer turned foreign aid consultant, and frequently wonders whether it's time for a new career. He's been traveling since birth, and has lived on five of seven continents, but the best place he's found is the Oregon coast. When he can, he makes his home there. In between journeys, he edits *Metaphorosis* magazine (https://magazine.metaphorosis.com/) and works on his own speculative stories of love and disaster. His story collection *Chambers of the Heart* came out in April 2022. Find out more **@BMorrisAllen** and https://www.bmorrisallen.com/.

In the Grip of Yesterday

P.A. Cornell

"Junkie piece o' shit!"

The words carry more force than the kick that splits my mouth. Still, it throws him off balance and I grab his ankle and pull him down to my level, literally. I know how these people see me. I get why they're kicking my ass. Docsn't mean I'll just lie here and take it.

His buddy grabs me by the jacket and lifts. I let him, pulling the switchblade from my pocket as I do. I've been jumped enough times—both by guys like them and guys like me—that I come prepared. I jerk around and hold it to his eye.

That's all it takes. That's all it usually takes. They start running, and I'm alone in the alley. I should head home but the craving won't let me. I give in; slide down the bricks to the ground where I retrieve the blister of Emosynth I scored just before those assholes showed up. I snap it in half and smear the clear liquid onto my arm. I work it in like it's lotion, and that's when the Nostalgia hits me.

It's her. Thank god. Last time it was just a piece of music I hadn't heard in a while. A nice memory, but nothing like my memories of Michelle. She smiles. Hair, lightened to a dark honey in the summer sun, falls over her face. She laughs at something I've said. "I love you," she says, surprising herself as much as me. We both laugh. I should've said it back. Why didn't I?

Nostalgia makes memories more vivid than when you lived through them the first time. That's how the drug gets you. The colours are brighter, the smells sweeter— her touch sends shockwaves across my body and all I can think is, *I love you...I love you.*

It wears off too soon. It seems soon, anyway, but night's given way to bright sun, and the streets are filled with noise. I get up, moaning as my body reminds me of the beating I took last night. Blood's crusted across my face and the front of my jacket. I check my teeth and confirm they're where they should be, then start the walk home, stares coming at me from all sides as people give me space on the sidewalk. I barely take in their scorn. Already, I'm thinking of my next hit.

When I get home there's two messages waiting. One from work, reminding me to come get my pink slip. I wouldn't bother, but they still owe me money and I need it. The pile of unpaid bills on my kitchen table needs reducing. But even as I think that I'm calculating how long I can survive without electricity, running water, heat. I play the next message. My sister Corey asking where I've been; how I am; if I'm coming to my niece's seventh birthday. *What day is it anyway?*

I go online to find out, but I'm sucked into my usual post-Nostalgia habit: creeping Michelle's socials. I check them daily. More like multiple times a day. She's all I think about. How could I have lived years not thinking of her once? Not until that first hit of Nostalgia.

Like most Emosynth users, I started with Joy. It's the most addictive, they say, but also the most socially acceptable. Soccer moms are popping Joy in public at their kids' games and no one gives a shit. *Of course* it wasn't going to be edgy enough for me. I had to try the other synthesized emotions. I made it through Fear and Listlessness, then hit on Nostalgia and never looked back.

Other synths wear off after a few hours, but Nostalgia lingers. I'm not in my memories anymore, but they're still in me. I smile. She's just posted a new selfie. I take it in. She sits in an armchair, next to an orange lamp. Behind her a painting of a dog. I focus on her face, noticing the lines it's acquired over the years. The eyes are the same. The hair dyed blonde but looking as soft as I remember. I can almost smell her shampoo.

My finger hovers over the 'send friend request' icon. As usual, I chicken out. It's been too long. No way she remembers me. *Fuck this.*

I head out in search of more Nostalgia.

The dealer's not even a little surprised to see me back so soon. He holds out my usual. I hold out my cash. The last of it, with no job to speak of. Can't exactly hold down a job when you can't stomach the present.

"Don't take it here," is all he says to me.

I snatch the blister from him, then walk just far enough away he won't complain. Two blocks at most. As I crack the blister, it's slapped free from my hand and the contents spill on the ground.

"Fuck!" I reach for it, thinking maybe I can lick it off the pavement when two arms reach around me. I turn to fight the assholes from last night but it's Corey. My switchblade's out and I'm holding it to her face. She doesn't flinch.

"You need help," she says, with both her voice and her eyes.

I look back at the pavement. The synth's soaked into the cracks and I wonder if pavement can get nostalgic. I envy that broken patch of dirty ground like I've never envied anything and I know, in that moment, Corey's right.

The rehab looks nice enough. They tell me they specialize in Emosynth addiction. I tune out after that. I try, but living in the moment gets harder with every hit. Your mind wanders, drifts backwards through time. I think again of Michelle. Then I see her.

This can't be. I didn't take the hit. But there she is, looking like the selfie from this morning. She stands in front of an armchair, next to a lamp. Behind her the dog painting. I realize the picture was taken here. And by the look on her face when she sees me, I *know* she's here for the same reason I am.

We just stare at each other for a while, then she smiles, just like she does in my memories. *I love you*, I think. *I love you*. And this time I walk over to tell her.

© 2022 P.A. Cornell

Science Fiction - 1059 words

About the Author

P.A. Cornell is a Chilean-Canadian writer who wrote her first speculative fiction story as a third-grade assignment, and still has it in her possession over three decades later. A member of SFWA and graduate of the Odyssey workshop, her short fiction has appeared in several professional anthologies and genre magazines. This is her third publication in *Cossmass Infinities*. For a full bibliography visit https://www.pacornell.com/.

Victorian Resistance & the Lords Insectile

M. Legree

Hurrying to an appointment, the young medical student Franken turned a street corner and almost ran into one of the Grigs on the sidewalk. The insect was an unusually large one, eight feet tall at least, and it had a man caught in its raptorial forelimbs and was dismembering him as casually as a diner unraveling a Chelsea bun. The policeman on the corner had turned his back, and pedestrians on the sidewalk were crossing to the other side of the street, their faces carefully blank.

After a moment, the Grig seemed to take notice of him. "Good day, sir," it said. It touched its blood-spattered forehead with one of its intermediate limbs in a seeming salute. The insect's voice was warm, avuncular. By modulating the airflow through the spiracles in their thoraces, they were remarkably adept at mimicking human speech.

Franken bent over and retched violently into the gutter. That night he joined the resistance.

————

Men in black cloaks and top hats crowded the surgical theater, all talking at once, like a great flock of crows come to roost. Invitations had specified the dress code, and the doorman handed out masks to the guests as they entered, so that now every man had his face concealed behind an effigy of Guy Fawkes.

Dr. Franken, standing in the well of the theater and wearing the same costume as his audience, surveyed the little crowd. The day was overcast. A murky light filtered down from the circular skylight overhead, and two gas jets bracketing the surgery lent the masked faces a ruddy luster.

"Looks a likely crowd, sir," said his assistant, Spivey, from behind him. The little mustached man was the only unmasked person in the theater, a colorful presence with his gold-threaded paisley waistcoat and white shirtsleeves.

Franken clapped his hands for attention. Slowly, the babble subsided into muttering and then silence. Franken waited until all eyes were upon him and sketched a bow. "Gentlemen, thank you for attending my little demonstration! You will forgive these theatrical flourishes, but I'm certain you can understand the need for anonymity—I assure you it will be worth your while."

Franken wore a surgeon's leather apron and gloves under his cloak. Before him was the operating table, its bulky occupant concealed beneath a sheet. He stepped forward, and—with a magician's flourish—yanked the cover away. There was a collective gasp from the audience.

Strapped to the table, prone and quiescent, was an insect. Standing, it would have been six feet tall, with the sallow, etiolated color of something found under a rock. Spivey handed him his heavy blackthorn walking stick. Franken drew a deep breath and tapped the prisoner insect on the head with the iron-shod ferrule; there was no reaction. He was suddenly glad that he was wearing a mask. He knew the creature's wicked mandibles had been filed down, and that it was sedated within an inch of its life, but the horror of its proximity still touched him.

"Most of you will be familiar with the standard insect body plan—the head, thorax, and...abdomen." He tapped the thing's distended gaster and moved on quickly. "They greatly resemble their smaller brethren, but there *are* differences." He tapped the elongated appendages at the posterior, something like an earwig's pincers. "These enlarged cerci enable them to counterfeit a bipedal gait.

The legs, since they are not required for locomotion, have been specialized: the posterior pair for lifting and grasping heavy objects; the intermediate pair, which are smaller and more delicate, for finer tasks." He paused to clear his throat. "This specimen has had its anterior limbs surgically removed." Spivey stepped forward and handed him one of the preserved arms. Cleaned and kiln-dried, it was about the size of a cricket bat, with a multitude of toothy points. Franken received it hesitantly, his hand trembling. "As you know, the Grigs are a subterranean species, with forelimbs adapted for digging—something like gigantic mole crickets. Their serrated forelimbs also make formidable weapons."

He shook his head to clear the memory and stepped forward hastily to hand the thing to a tall man in the front row. The tall man glanced at it and passed it to his neighbor, a dumpy figure with the black, broken nails of a coal heaver, who showed much greater interest.

"Blimey!" exclaimed the workman, feeling the sharpness of the serrations with a calloused fingertip. "That would gut a bugger, wouldn't it, then?"

Franken sneered instinctively, once again glad for the mask. He reminded himself that an army required soldiers of all ranks. But he so detested the necessity of dealing with the lower classes!

"May I inquire," said the tall man, "how you obtained this...specimen?" He spoke in the cultured drawl of one born into privilege. The contrast with his neighbor could not have been more obvious.

"Certainly," said Franken. He hesitated. He had almost added *My Lord*. How did one address a person whose rank you did not know—or, at least, were not supposed to know? He decided it was best not to make any assumptions and went on quickly. "The Grigs are no more immune to chasing the dragon than our own lower classes."

"And you plan to liberate our government by…promoting an addiction to opium?" The tall man's skepticism was evident even through his disguise.

Franken shook his head. "Gentlemen!" He had to raise his voice to cut through the babel.

The trophy was still making its rounds, and the audience returned its attention to him only reluctantly. "I did not invite you here to give you a lesson in insect anatomy but to unveil a new weapon against our oppressors. Observe!"

Spivey had drawn a stiletto from his boot and, with its point, he pried at the juncture of two segments of the insect's swollen belly. Something white and bulbous pushed out suddenly, and Spivey flinched backward. The onlookers gasped again.

"A parasite," continued Franken. "This specimen has been infested by a species of stylopid fly. You see here the adult female, which is vermiform, with no legs and no eyes. She has only a mouth, with which she consumes the Grig from within—"

Someone shouted a ribald comment from the back of the room, and there was a ripple of laughter in response. Franken ignored the interruption.

"Stylopids normally must be studied with a magnifying glass, but I have raised these in my laboratory—forced them, really, like hothouse vegetables—to a fittingly monstrous size. Now," he nodded at Spivey again, and the little man stepped forward once more. This time he plunged the knife in and tore the Grig open. The sedated insect spasmed once and did not move again.

The stylopid female was squirming in its death agony, but a dozen busy forms, hand-sized, had spilled from the dead insect's abdomen and began crawling about the tabletop. The men of the audience were shouting now. Franken stepped forward and began picking them up, one by one, and depositing them into the big glass jar Spivey had taken from under the table.

"Her larvae!" shouted Franken, holding one of them up. The thing was dead white, like its parent, and the size of his hand, with six hooked appendages. He was careful to keep its mouthparts away from his glove. The parasite's saliva had the property of dissolving chitin—the better to invade its host's exoskeleton—but it worked tolerably well on cowhide too.

"Even tonight they will be distributed among the opium dens of the East End, and the plague will begin!"

The theater was in an uproar. Franken could make no sense of the cacophony, but the aristocratic man in the front row beckoned, and Franken stepped forward and cupped a hand to his ear.

"Hardly sporting, is it?" said the tall man.

Franken drew back, angered in spite of himself, and bit back a retort. Was it *sporting* when the Lords Insectile emptied our workhouses of the poor and herded them into the tunnels under London, to emerge years later as unholy hybrids—pithecines, vulpines, corvines, and others—created by God-knew-what profane process?

He was still attempting to frame a suitable reply when a scream pierced the general bedlam, and all heads turned to the double doors at the head of the theater stairs. A dozen gray figures, wearing the livery of the Domestic Mandate, had emerged there and were leaping down into the seats, wielding truncheons. Blood sprayed as a man near the back row was brained; another lost his footing and vanished under the tide of panicked audience members fleeing for the exits.

Spivey seized him by the arm. "It's the pithies, sir!" he shouted. "Time to scarper!"

Franken hesitated. He was half-minded to stay and fight, and his thumb found the catch hidden in the pommel of his walking stick, preparatory to drawing forth the hidden blade. But Spivey was shouting and tugging at his elbow, and he knew the little man was right. Together, they turned and hurried out of the theater, Franken with the jar of larval parasites tucked under his arm. Spivey slammed shut the door leading from the surgical well and threw the bolt.

"That'll hold 'em but a moment, sir. Make for the back door."

Franken nodded. They fled down a short, twisting passage that opened onto an alleyway, where his hansom waited. He had but a moment to wonder at the carelessness of the pithecines at leaving an unguarded exit. But then—unlike their masters—they were not known for their cunning. They were only half-human, after all.

Then they were outside, boots clattering on the cobbles. Franken had thrown off his mask and was reaching to undo the clasp of his cloak when he saw something dropping down at him from above and behind: The pithecines had not left the back way unguarded after all. Two of the simians had been hanging from the building like spiders, waiting to pounce.

There were two sharp reports, and then the thud of something heavy hitting the pavement.

Franken unclasped the cloak and cast it aside. Spivey was holding a smoking revolver, its barrel pointing straight up. Franken toed one of the bodies on the street and it flopped over onto its back. There was a bullet hole between the beetling brows.

"Good show, Spivey."

"If I may be so bold, sir—time we should be going!"

Franken nodded again. He could still hear screams from inside the theater.

Spivey was already untethering the horse, an old gray nag that had hardly blinked at the gunfire. Franken climbed into the passenger compartment, clutching the jar with its squirming contents against his chest. Spivey mounted the driver's seat and snapped the reins. In a moment, they had exited the alley and pulled out into traffic. Franken heard the little man heave a sigh of relief.

He frowned and threw open the communicating trap door. "Make haste, Spivey! We have deliveries to make!"

© 2022 M. Legree

Science Fantasy - 1868 words

About the Author

Chained to a desk during the day, M. Legree is released at dusk to write genre fiction. He lives alone in a Depression-era bungalow overlooking the subtropical bayous in the historical East End of Houston, Texas, guarded by a pack of savage mongrels. Living in the past, Legree prefers to reread the old tales of Nathaniel Hawthorne, H. G. Wells, and Sir Arthur Conan Doyle. He often combines his interests in history and cryptozoology to create his stories.

Seraph in Ruins

Mere Rain

The old military installation was like something out of a horror film: endless convoluted corridors filled with skeletons and shattered furniture, blood-stained walls, black doorways through which unstoppable monsters lunged without warning.

Seraph was used to it.

She knew the landmarks: turn right at the two-headed serpent mummy to shortcut to the radiation lab, start running at the acid-spattered area to make the jump over the bottomless pit, spiderborgs often hide behind those dead ferns. She was tough and well-armed. She could see in the dark.

She was one of the monsters.

But a solitary monster. Whatever the quartet of vampires was hunting in the adjacent corridor was nothing to do with her. Those bloodsuckers weren't her friends, or her enemies, or even her kind, although most people might not recognize the difference. Whoever had been dumb enough to come down here to be eaten wasn't her kind, either.

She hissed irritably under her breath. Stupid.

Stupid humans and their stupid destructive impulses. Anyone stupid enough to come here deserved to be vamp snacks. It wasn't her problem. None of it was her problem, anymore.

She cursed silently at herself as she changed course to intercept the vampires.

Already she could smell the stink of rotten blood and unwashed flesh. These vampires must've been fails, the unfortunates who lost their minds when they were changed, becoming violent animals driven only by the thirst. They were easier to kill than the vampires who retained their human rationality, although just as physically intimidating. They were many times stronger and faster than a human.

Not as strong or as fast as Seraph, of course. They were just transfused; Seraph was engineered. There had been several attempts at super soldiers over the years; why the addition of vampirism had been judged a sound choice she had no idea. Things had been kind of crazy at the end of the war—a losing war for all sides, it had been clear by then. And afterward, no one involved was left alive to ask.

Seraph ought to have been dead, too, but apparently, vampires didn't age, just like in the movies. Not that they had movies anymore.

Seraph could smell the bitter, dead odor of vampire blood. No nourishment there, which is why they didn't turn on one another. The human they were hunting must have gotten a cut in. Proof, if she'd had any doubt, that these bloodsuckers were the mindless sort.

They weren't even smart enough to consider that Seraph, not being their prey, might pose a threat. They didn't turn from their pursuit until she had ripped the head off the slowest vamp. Decapitation was fatal unless someone stuck the head back on right away and did something to keep it in place while it reattached. The dead one's companions didn't try, if they even knew to. They just turned and launched themselves howling at Seraph.

The first one to reach her got her saber across its throat and collapsed. One of the remaining two, the one that stank of blood, ran for a side passage. Apparently, one wound was enough for today. Seraph didn't chase it.

The one that had been in the lead was the largest, probably the strongest, a bald man with bull shoulders and a thick neck. He lunged toward Seraph, staggering as something struck him in the back. He spun, looking for the threat, then spun again as Seraph moved toward him. This close, she could have been on him in the blink of an eye, but she didn't want the human taking her for one of the predators and shooting her with that projectile weapon. Not that it was likely to do any serious damage to her body, but a good leather jacket like this wasn't easy to come by these days.

Anyway, she hadn't had a good claw-to-claw fight in a long time.

And she still didn't get one today. She easily dodged a couple swipes and smacked her opponent when she could have ripped out his throat, in case he needed a minute to get into dueling form. Then training and annoyance took over and she eviscerated him.

Then it was just her looking through the darkness at a young woman who had at least the sense to come down here with a jury-rigged pair of old night goggles.

She was slim and tan-complected, with short black hair that the goggles caused to stick out in different directions. Cute, in a grubby, waifish sort of way. Fashion and hygiene had declined a lot in the past century. Seraph had gotten used to it.

The young woman had lived a lot fewer years, but apparently enough to get used to people who dripped blood from their claws. She didn't take a shot at Seraph, anyhow. Sensible, grateful, cautious? Who knew.

"What are you doing down here, kid?" Seraph asked.

The woman relaxed visibly—well, not to most eyes, but perceptibly to Seraph's enhanced senses—at the sound of Seraph's husky, well-modulated voice.

"The water pump broke. I thought I might find a replacement part in the mechanical plant."

It wasn't that dumb, although most of the usable pieces had been stripped years ago.

"That was a big risk, for not much chance of success," she remarked.

The girl shrugged. "No pump, we all get cholera and die."

"This place has more monsters than spare parts. You should head back topside."

"Folks in town really need this."

"Not my problem."

"Why'd you save me, then?"

"Just preserving resources for myself. Too many predators is a drain on the ecosystem."

"You gonna eat me, then?" The woman's voice was challenging.

Seraph moved faster than the human eye could follow. The woman clawed futilely at the hand around her neck. Sensibly, she quickly abandoned that and reached for the knife on her belt. Seraph caught her wrist before she could draw it.

"I could," Seraph whispered in her ear. She licked the grimy cheek, tasting fear. "Only I'm not hungry." It had been true a minute ago but wasn't now. "Next time I find you down here, you're dinner. Go."

Seraph released the girl and vanished into the darkness. Maybe she waited there, listening to make sure the idiot got out safely, but the woman had no way to know that.

She couldn't know, either, that, when instead of heading for the surface she continued on her way to the lab and spent an hour scavenging parts, nervously looking over her shoulder every other minute, Seraph was outside the door, standing in the darkness, making sure nothing dangerous came her way.

It was only time. Seraph had plenty of that.

She had saved the girl's life. She had made certain that she and her bits of machinery got safely back to town. That was more than enough. More than she owed anyone. There was no reason for Seraph to give her even a passing thought.

It was only from boredom that she kept an eye out for the girl with the tool belt.

———

She found her a day and a half later, using a sand-filled depression as a casting mold.

Since the girl was working with molten metal, Seraph refrained from startling her, watching from the shadows as she poured the glowing-hot liquid into the hand-made form. When she had finished and set aside the heated crucible, Seraph remarked, "Nice work."

The girl jumped and came around holding her gun, although she kept her finger off the trigger. "Who's there?" she called, her voice mostly even.

Of course, human eyes would have trouble adjusting from the intense light of the glowing ore. Not shooting at a voice in the dark was unusual respect for life, these days.

"It's your knight in anti-shine armor," she told the girl.

The girl's face stayed blank.

"The vampire bitch who saved your ass in the underground," Seraph clarified.

"Oh! Um, hi." The girl's voice was a little scratchy with tension, but she didn't smell excessively of fear. "Thanks again for that."

"What are you doing out here?"

"Oh. You were right about the lab being pretty well picked over. But I found the materials to make substitute parts."

"Why out here?" Seraph waved a hand at the darkness, the irregular hills made of sand and ash and shattered homes.

"In case something exploded."

"Oh. Good thinking, kid."

"I'm not a kid."

"You got a name, kid?"

The girl rolled her eyes. "Yai. How about you?"

"I'm Seraph."

"Seraph." She rolled it in her mouth. "That's an old word, isn't it? How old are you?"

Seraph snorted. "I was probably older when the war started than you are now. Sixteen?"

"I'm *twenty*," the girl said with the outrage of youth.

"Nineteen and a half," Seraph murmured. As the girl spluttered, Seraph spoke over her. "Okay, okay, twenty. All grown up. Years of engineering experience."

"I do have years of engineering experience," Yai said sulkily.

It was probably true. People grew up fast since the war. No years of school, no weekends of television and slumber parties, no summers at the beach. And her machining work looked solid, anyway. Seraph had picked up a good general knowledge over the decades.

"Okay," Seraph half-apologized. "I believe you. You ready to flip the switch?"

"There's not a switch, the engine has to be—anyway, no, I need to finish assembling it."

"Mind if I hang around?"

"What for?"

"Figure I might learn something, you being such a hotshot engineer and all." Seraph could smell the pungence of saber-toothed puma nearby. They probably wouldn't try to take the girl while Seraph was lurking.

"Suit yourself," Yai said, turning back to her parts. Her shoulders hunched a little as she turned her back on the shadows, but only a little, and they mostly relaxed as she focused on her work.

After a couple minutes of silence—well, silence for Yai, Seraph could hear quite a few things—the girl asked, "What was that before, about the night not shining?"

"Huh? Oh, no, that was knight with a K. Uh, it was a historical type of warrior."

"From the war?"

Seraph repressed a laugh. "No, years before that. Hundreds of years ago, actually, before guns and machinery and stuff."

"I never thought about that. People must've been like animals once."

"We are animals, we just have better technology. Knights were the advanced weaponry of their time. They were supposed to have this code of honor, protecting the weak and rescuing ladies and serving their countries, but that's probably just a story."

"So you were a knight?"

"What? No, I'm not that old."

"But you were the advanced technology of your time, right? And you fought for your country in the war, and you rescued me the other day."

Well, damn. Hard to argue with that.

Seraph heard one puma cough to its mate, a low warning. A few seconds later she heard the engine growl that had alerted the cats.

"Shut off the light and put out the fire," Seraph ordered.

The girl was already reaching for the sand pail and flicking off the spotlight as she asked, "How come?"

"Got a friend with a dune buggy?"

"No."

Seraph put a hand on the girl's elbow, feeling her jump at the touch in the dark. "Move away from the fire pit. In case they have night vision."

"My pump," Yai protested as she let Seraph lead her away.

"I won't let them take it. We're moving to a better position for attack. Let me know when you can hear the engine."

Yai tilted her head to the night. "I can."

"Okay. Keep quiet. We're behind a dune. I hope the residual heat in the sand will be enough to disguise us."

Yai fumbled her goggles out of the belt loop without trying to shake her arm free of Seraph's grip. "It should," she whispered. "I only see a glow above the work station and a shimmer following their vehicle."

"Right. You got a night-sight on that pistol?"

"Of course."

"Can you lay down some cover and not hit me?"

"No problem. You're way cooler than a normal person."

Seraph allowed herself a small, private grin at that unintentional compliment, but didn't reply because she was trying to hear the men in the buggy. They didn't seem to be saying anything, just hooting and shouting.

Intimidation noise, like monkeys, she thought contemptuously.

"The Ramblas Hill Crew," Yai whispered. "They've been trying to strongarm us into giving them supplies in exchange for protection."

Seraph nodded. She hadn't been paying attention to the little town and its affairs lately, but the protection racket was as old as human nature.

The hooting faded a little when the gang realized there was no one in sight. One man called, "Come out, come out wherever you are!" and got a sprinkle of laughter.

Another man, deeper voiced, shouted, "Come out now and we'll go easy on ya, girlie! We know who ya are! We seen ya at the repair station! Don't make us come lookin' for ya!"

Yai had gone a little pale.

"Any objection to me just killing the fuck out of these assholes?" Seraph whispered.

"Hell, no," Yai breathed. "Wait a sec, though."

She took what looked like a handful of sticks out of a pouch attached to her belt. They unfolded into one long stick with a tiny screen at one end. Yai poked the other end out from behind the dune and a grainy thermal image of six men milling around a vehicle appeared on the little screen.

"Damn," Seraph breathed. She hadn't seen tech like this in decades. "Where'd you find this scope?"

"Made it out of spare parts."

"Color me impressed, baby engineer."

Yai didn't reply, but Seraph could tell that she was smiling.

Seraph waited for Yai to put away her viewing device, "I'm going over the dune, to the right. On the count of three, I want you to take a shot at the men on the left. Be fast. Don't worry about hitting them, just get back behind the dune before they have time to get a bead on you. Got it? One, two—"

Seraph launched herself over the dune. The move wouldn't have been possible for a normal person: the sand would have crumbled and slipped under their feet. Seraph didn't touch the surface, clearing the obstacle in a single bound. The gang wasn't expecting an attack from above. They were scattering, eyes slewed to the man who was screaming and clutching his punctured stomach.

Seraph clawed out the closest man's throat before he even noticed her. The next one she kicked in the knee. He collapsed with a high shriek, leg bent the wrong way. The man behind him turned and ran.

She feinted at the coward to make sure he fled in the right direction, which was to say the direction of pumas, who were loitering a quarter-mile away in hopes of picking up an easy meal, then spun back to dodge a bullet from a scar-headed man who was probably the leader. He was the biggest and had the largest gun. Her dodge brought her close to a weaselly-faced man with a machete. She slapped the weapon out of weaselly's hand and smashed his nose into his brain, then threw his twitching body at scar-head.

Scar-head went down under his compatriot's weight, and she was on top of him before he could push the corpse aside. She kicked the gun out of his hand and stamped on his throat with a crunch of vertebrae, surveying the field of battle for any continued risks. Nothing moved but the man she had knee-capped, trying to crawl inconspicuously away.

She strolled after him and broke his wrist.

"Looks clear," Yai called, only a little tremor in her voice.

"Affirmative. You can come out now."

Yai approached cautiously, scanning the fallen as she passed.

"Allow me to present you with this fine dune buggy as the spoils of war, milady," Seraph said, bowing.

Yai's face lit up. "You really don't want it? I could just use it to move the pump, then give it back."

"How did you get that thing out here in the first place?"

"I sledded it, in pieces. This will be much easier."

"Let's get moving, then. These bastards will attract all sorts of nasties soon enough." She picked up the smaller corpse at her feet and tossed it away from Yai's work. She pried the gun out of scar-head's cooling hand and unbuckled his belt, which held a long knife of reasonable quality, a Swiss Army knife, and a two-foot wrench. Then she tossed him after his mate.

"What about him?" Yai tilted her delicate chin at the crippled thug, who was still worming slowly toward the darkness. Not that he'd have much chance out there.

"I was saving him for breakfast," Seraph admitted.

"Oh." Yai looked nonplussed only for a second. "Do you want to eat him now, so we don't have to watch him?"

Seraph had worked up quite an appetite. "It wouldn't bother you? I can wait."

"He dies the same whether I see it or not, right? And these a-holes are just as dead. Something'll come for the carrion like you said. Everything's gotta eat."

Yai turned to inspect her now-cool metal-casting, not looking as Seraph bit into the wounded man's throat.

Blood was food for her. She didn't usually kill to get it, but she had no intention of leaving any of these bastards alive. From the darkness came distant screams as the pumas found their dinner.

Seraph scrubbed blood from her face with her victim's shirt and went to lift the heavier parts into the dune buggy. She found Yai's sled, which was made from an old car hood. Skinny kid must have some solid muscles if she had dragged all this here on her own.

"That went a lot faster," Yai murmured as she screwed the last of the smaller components together. "Thanks."

"Sure thing. See you around, kid."

Yai bit her lip for a moment. "Yeah. See you."

She put the buggy in motion and headed for the dim lights of town. Seraph stood in the blood-reeking darkness and listened until the sound of the engine died away.

———

In the movies, vampires couldn't go out in the sunlight. Seraph hadn't had the chance to test that; by the time they had changed her, years of bombardment and environmental sabotage had left the atmosphere permanently obscure. The blue skies and ocean of her childhood were a distant, cherished memory. They were mostly what she had to value these days, memories.

But maybe not the only thing.

The underground base had a pool, still full of water. It was too laced with heavy metal contaminants to be useful to regular humans, but it was safe for Seraph. She carefully scrubbed all the blood off her leathers, and then took a bath.

Studying her blurred, sallow reflection in a stainless-steel door as she finger-combed her cropped black hair smooth, she had a sudden memory of her Abuela murmuring, *Que bonita, angelita*, as she combed Seraph's long hair. Ribbons, a pink party dress with white lace…

"Hah," Seraph breathed out. She rubbed clawed hands over her black-clad arms. Not pretty or an angel now. And no one was inviting her to this party.

In town, the inhabitants were celebrating the repaired water pump with an impromptu festival: music and dancing and shared food. Seraph could smell hot corn oil and beer. Two guitars and a hand drum played *Marieta*. She leaned against a shadowed wall and listened.

She was well out of sight of the fiesta, but after a few minutes, she heard footsteps coming her way.

"Hey," Yai said softly. "I'm glad you're here. This ought to be your party."

"I doubt too many people would be pleased to see me."

"I told them how you helped me. They're real happy to hear half the Ramblas are gone. They're talking about maybe getting a posse together to get back Eng and Millie's daughter that was took last month. We might have a chance now."

Seraph had taken a vow once to die to defend her nation.

That nation hadn't existed in a long time.

"I suppose I could make time to kill a few more of those thugs," Seraph remarked, casual-like.

"Yeah?"

"It's good to finish what you start."

Yai leaned against the wall a foot away. "I don't think I said last night, but that fight—you were pretty amazing."

"Designed that way," Seraph said modestly. "And plenty of practice."

"They say you were a soldier."

The girl hadn't made that connection before. "You been asking about me?" Seraph asked, letting a teasing note creep into her voice. Rustily.

The girl scowled and ducked her head. "Knowledge is power," she quoted.

It was a slogan that had been stale before Seraph's time. *Knowing is half the battle.* That was a line from something from her childhood. Something she had watched on television. How many years had it been since the last television broadcast?

G.I. Joe. Seraph's first crush had been on a woman on that show. A brunette with short hair and guns.

"When's this daring attack scheduled?"

"Well, Eng and Millie want to go tomorrow. But Sheriff Lopez thinks the Ramblas may threaten to kill Nenia if they see us coming."

"He's probably right," Seraph said absently, thinking about the layout of Ramblas Hill. "I'll scope it out tonight. See the lay of the land, what kind of security they have."

"That would help a lot." Yai gave her a quick look. "I asked Greta the book lady about knights. She said the lady was supposed to give the knight a favor, but she didn't know what that was."

"I don't know, either," Seraph admitted. "Something for luck, I guess."

"Oh. Well, for luck." Yai planted a quick, clumsy kiss on the corner of Seraph's mouth, then ran back to the party.

Seraph watched her go, grinning until her fangs cut her lip.

As Seraph headed uphill, she could hear the guitarist begin a song that had been old when she was young, praising the dark-haired girl of her heart.

————

The next morning she was warned of her damsel's approach by the cheerful growl of the dune buggy. It sounded like Yai had cleaned the air filter, and probably adjusted the valve train.

Yai found her in a remarkably short time.

Seraph was lying on the crude but comfortable slab bed she had made for her underground lair. Yai sat beside her.

"Didn't I tell you it was dangerous down here?" Seraph asked without opening her eyes.

"I figured I was safe enough while you were around."

Seraph opened her eyes. Cute, tough, little baby engineer. "Probably," she allowed.

"Did you hear the bell ringing?"

"I heard it." When Seraph was a child they had rung it for weddings and funerals, and on Sundays to remind people to come to Mass. *Give thanks.*

"It was celebration for getting Nenia back."

"It okay that I left Consuela and Milo there, too?" The Ramblas' other young slaves had said that the gang had killed the rest of their family.

"Sure. They're staying with Nenia's parents for now."

"Good."

"Consuela said you killed everyone there."

"Yes." Seraph had drunk more blood than she needed. Now she felt both energized and relaxed.

"That was nice of you."

Seraph laughed. "Nice, huh?"

"Well, you know. Valiant. That word was in Greta's knight book," Yai added. "Along with favor. Anyway, I was thinking you deserved a reward."

Seraph studied her face. Yai was dark enough not to blush, but Seraph could feel the heat of blood rising to her cheeks.

"What did you have in mind, baby engineer?"

"I'm not a baby," Yai said. "And whatever you want."

"Anything?" Seraph stroked her throat, carefully to touch her with fingertips and not claws. Yai shivered, and not with fear.

"Don't you know a vampire's bite can be addictive?" Seraph admonished. "You might find yourself hooked."

Yai glanced at her, a meaningful under-the-lashes look that Seraph had seen many times over the decades, although rarely directed at her scary-ass self. "Would it be so bad if I kept coming back?"

"Mm." Seraph brushed her lips lightly along the girl's throat. "Let's see if I can make you want to come back for other reasons. Yai."

"About that favor…" Yai said meaningfully.

Her knight kissed her.

Science Fiction - 4080 words

About the Author

Mere Rain is an international nonentity of mystery whose library resides in California. Mere likes travel, food, art, mythology, and you. Feel free to reach out on social media. Mere has published short speculative fiction with *Other Worlds Ink*, *Mischief Corner*, *JMS Books*, *The Mad Scientist Journal*, and *Mythical Girls*. Find them on Twitter **@mere_rain**.

The Long Way Home

Tina S. Zhu

— June 5, 1977 — San Francisco —

Dearest Ying,

I'm in San Francisco, on the exact block you live on—just a few decades too early. Isn't that wild? In thirty-seven years, three months, and two days, we will meet. You will be practicing the aria *E amore un ladroncello* with your window open. I will listen from the sidewalk and holler through the open window that I like your voice. You will close the window, believing that is the last you will hear from me. But alas! I will rearrange my morning jog to stop by the coffee shop next door, and we will have a serendipitous encounter in thirty-seven years, three months, and two weeks. On our first date, you will call me well-traveled. I will say you have no idea. You will ask me where I come from. I will munch on my blueberry scone and not reply. In thirty-eight years, three months, and two days, we will celebrate our first anniversary at the same coffee shop. In thirty-nine years and two days, we will fight. You will storm off and tell me I can't keep leaving you behind after I run into Ba where Market and 2nd meet, and after three long days, you will forgive me after I come bearing roses to the premiere of *La Bohème*.

Fun fact! There is no coffee shop in 1977. There is, however, a laundromat. I bumped into your parents, who were on a date and passing by. I tried throwing a pebble at your mom, but as usual, she didn't notice me. As for your dad, though, I'm pretty sure he thought I was crazy or a ghost. Me asking what he thought of his future daughter dating me didn't help. Wonder what my dad, a David Bowie fanatic, would have said—bet he was listening to Ziggy Stardust on his final trip.

How are you? How is 2017?

Yours, Sofia Kang

— September 18, 1635 — Croatia —

Hello from Croatia!

I can't picture you here, so far outside the fog of San Francisco. Speaking of which, thanks for the photo and the fresh dark roast coffee beans! The aroma of fresh twenty-first-century coffee is much appreciated in any century. It was wonderful hearing that my last letter was a pleasant surprise. Your story about the coworker who believes he's the next Pavarotti was something—I could almost hear you relaying your best imitation of the coworker's singing voice over the sound of the waves.

To answer your question whether I'll be back for your birthday and your long-awaited Big Sur trip in September, the honest answer is I don't know. I don't know when I'll be back, but let me reassure you I will not be wandering through time forever in search of a ghost. I don't believe in ghosts. The time-jumping tendencies of us Kangs don't persist after death—we were watchmakers, not gods. We have too much fun, living fast and dying young despite having unlimited time.

As for me, I'm traveling to understand what was so wonderful about time jumping that made Ba want to leave me and my mother behind, leaving me to learn the fine art of time-jumping from my grandmother's journals. In the endless olive fields and boat-filled ports, a mere hundred nautical miles from where my dad disappeared in 1583, I'm no closer to answering the question that started my quest, the one he says I must find the answer to before it's too late. Before the Kang line will be gone for good.

You mentioned rehearsals are ramping up again, but if you have time, send me a scone from that coffee shop through the time capsule on that tree with the wilting leaves in the park—that park on top of the hill, the one with the stairs you hate.

Sofia

P.S. I noticed you underlined the date on your postcard—sorry, I didn't realize it's 2018 and not 2017 in the present. I haven't been keeping track, not like you.

— April 23, 1992 — Chile —

I'm here at the end of the world. More precisely, at the southernmost lighthouse in the world, the Monumental Cabo de Hornos in Cape Horn, Chile. This was one of the few places on his list he didn't visit. There's nothing explaining why he wanted to stop here. Was it for the penguins? You would have liked the penguins. The lighthouse itself is this red building on a ridge, standing alone against the relentless tides and gale-force winds. This lighthouse, a monument to all the sailors who have passed away making the treacherous journey, was only finished last November but will be rebuilt again in 2006. Maybe that's why Ba wanted to visit—to visit the original before time swept it away as it does everything else.

You haven't replied to my last postcard. I'm getting worried. Are you busy with rehearsals, or am I worrying you by traveling to such remote places? I only have a few stops left. Next time I'm in 2018, I'll show you everything I've collected from my journey.

I'll be in SF soon. No idea what day of the week or time of day (I never did master that level of precision when jumping), but I'll be there.

See you soon, Sofia

— August 25, 2018 — San Francisco —

Dear Ying,

I'm delivering this final postcard to San Francisco, to your front door and in person for your birthday.

I tried to aim for today to surprise you, but I landed a day too early. I saw you at the park yesterday afternoon, sitting next to the baby redwood Ba planted with the birdhouse time capsule hanging from its trunk. You were holding a scone from the coffee shop. I couldn't see the scone itself but recognized the crinkle of the paper bag as you were redoing your smudged eyeliner. I wasn't sure if you wanted to see me right before your performance last night, so I kept my distance.

Do you want to know what Ba's challenge was? He told me to figure out where home is before it's too late. Before I end up like him. This is coming from a man who made it to my fifth birthday but didn't come back until my fifteenth. Ba met his untimely end on the high seas, my grandmother in the Great Fire of Rome. Unlike them, I'm not destined for such a spectacular end. I have collected countless stories and observed countless people with no luck finding somewhere to belong. I'm a Kang. We spend our lives never rooted to a single time, with freedom from the ultimate constraint that binds everyone else, but Kangs never belong. We find joy in being perpetual strangers, laughing at everyone else's inability to experience what is easy for us.

But I figured it out. I figured out where I belong by discovering what wasn't there in my travels—the rests in songs, the times to catch your breath you told me are what make music different from white noise. Blame the lighthouse. The gray waters churned underneath the observation deck of the lighthouse as I held up the photo of you laughing on the pier, and it was then I realized where I wanted to be. I ran outside, ripped it up, and threw away the rest of Ba's list into the water, letting the water sweep away the fragments. Perhaps next week in Big Sur, we will stumble upon a paper scrap that has traveled all the way from Cape Horn for twenty-six years. Perhaps we will frame it in your living room as evidence for posterity.

If you fear learning where I belong, if you fear that I'll be running through time for the rest of my life, don't. Do you want to know where I'll be? Finish reading, and I'll tell you.

Yours, Sofia Kang

© 2022 Tina S. Zhu

Science Fiction - 1375 words

About the Author

Tina has work forthcoming in *Fireside Magazine*. When she's not writing code or stories, she can be found in bookstores or eating dim sum in California. Find her on Twitter **@tinaszhu**.

Love Like Chocolate

Risa Wolf

The first flavor Sonora gave to me was delight. We'd crossed paths on the 72nd subway stairs a few days after our first date. I was full-on butterflies when I saw her, her face lit up with that sunbeam smile. She reached over the railing and caught my hand.

"Kari! I'm getting my new dog. Wanna come?"

The rescue was a few blocks away. She squeaked when the clumsy bundle of black and white spots bumbled up to her, wagging his tail so hard he could barely stand. Her eyes widened as he climbed into her lap, and when she turned to me, I swear I saw hearts dancing there. Hearts dripping with honey candy. And that's when I kissed

Sonora the first time. When I first drank deep from her sweetness and tasted the citrus honey flavor of it.

I wish I could say how sorry I am. I didn't know.

————

Sonora looked a bit like her namesake: spiky strawberry blonde hair like sunset on sand cliffs, dark dusty green eyes in gold-pale skin. She had one crooked tooth in front that made her smiles infectious. When I first spotted her at The Strand, she was wearing neon orange lipstick and a single dagger earring and I couldn't keep from staring. I don't know why she looked over at me. She kept my gaze for a second with a blank face, then winked before turning back to the person talking to her.

"She was gawping at me," she'd say, whenever someone asked how we'd met.

We had a patter, by then. "I did not gawp. I was chewing gum."

She'd raise her pierced eyebrow. "Does it matter?" Reaching out for my hand. "We met each other, didn't we? Whatever you did, it worked."

————

New York City was always filled with excitement. It didn't matter where I went: people enjoyed the city at every hour, leaving traces of themselves behind. I probably spent my life, pre-Sonora, taking in people's ambient essences without realizing it. My friends were never that affectionate, so I didn't notice anything unusual. Even my family wasn't demonstrative.

Everything changed, because of Sonora's kiss. I felt...sated, for the first time. Relaxed.

Sonora seemed to want more, too. "I don't know what it is," she murmured the first night I stayed over, the streetlight sneaking through the tatty blinds to scatter like sprinkles on her blue bedspread. "I can't get enough of you. You're so...soothing."

"Soothing?" I'd smirked. "Really? Never been accused of that before."

"I'm serious, jerk." She'd pinched me, then snuggled into my shoulder. "The moment I kiss you, I know everything is going to be all right. It's like whatever's tense inside me is slowly draining away."

That's when I had my first inkling. Of what I was doing to people. What I was.

Who wants to think they're a literal monster, though? I mean, how do you get help for something like this? How do you even describe it? Excuse me, do you eat emotions? If so, is there a way you can do it ethically?

So I hid myself in the romance of it all.

At this point, all I can do is try to give back to her.

That's all I can do.

————

The first night in the hospital, Sonora was given oxygen. "This really sucks," she coughed. "I feel like I've been hollowed out."

"Hollowed out? That's a bit on the nose, doncha think?"

She looked down at her stomach, concave where it used to have a soft pudge I loved to nuzzle. "It's not so bad, is it?"

I tilted my head, shoved a hunk of black hair out of my eyes. "Nothing about you could ever be bad, baby."

She rolled her eyes. "You're just saying that because you love me."

"Maybe. But it's your fault for loving me back."

When Sonora first told me she loved me, I didn't believe her. I didn't believe love could taste that bitter.

Little did I know.

————

Bitter flavors and I never got along. I hated the flavor of coffee and any salad with a hint of arugula or radicchio went straight to the garbage. I loved cocoa, though, so I was surprised when I bought cacao nibs and they were so sharply bitter I couldn't even keep them in my mouth. I thought I'd bought something else by mistake. I discovered later what it takes to make chocolate into what gets sold to us, how the beans are fermented for a week or more and then dried, then roasted, et cetera. It takes pressure and grinding and tempering to make cacao into the delectable confection so many people adore.

When I learned that, it put Sonora's kisses in a whole different light.

I think about it a lot these days: how much work it takes to make chocolate a synonym for sweetness.

————

Ben was my first boyfriend. It was one of those *I like you, sorta* things that pre-teens do. He tried to hold my hand once, but I told him I didn't like it, that his hands were sweaty. I know now it was that I hated his bland funk. Sorry, Ben.

Allison was my first girlfriend. I adored her dark, haunted eyes and the way in which she would sing about her pain. "God is cruel, and God doesn't care about any of us," she'd sing, and only now do I understand how much I reveled in that tart, mineral-soaked anguish. Sorry, Allie.

Gera was my first non-gendered lover and an LGBTIA activist. Ze had pastel rainbow hair I'd help zir dye every other month. I adored zir passionate anger–I can summon the umami succulence of it now that I look back. I even remember the hot zing of hate from the counter-protesters. I don't know if I subconsciously escalated things. I hope I didn't. Sorry, Gera.

If Sonora ever gets better, maybe I can make amends to them as well.

————

The interesting fact about bitter things is that they never *smell* bitter. They smell like something else. Sometimes roasty, sometimes green. So in the first throes of it, Sonora's love would surge, I'd catch a whiff of something warm and rich, and then she'd lean in to kiss me. The moment our lips touched, I'd get the bitterness, tongue-curlingly fierce.

I pulled away in disgust for a few weeks; I admit it. But Sonora didn't get angry. She'd twist her lip in that mischievous way she had and snicker "What's wrong baby, I got bad breath?"

I laughed a lot back then, gasping as Sonora chased me around the apartment trying to breathe on me, Charlie the dog yapping happily behind us. The sweetness of joy made it okay, made the flavor endurable.

But I still didn't believe love could taste so harsh. Not yet.

————

When the nurses asked me to leave so they could change Sonora's sheets and give her a bath, I stood outside in the hallway, where the air was the burned-hair smell of fright and the zippy basil tang of compassion. That's when my brain started to eat itself with questions.

Have I tried hard enough?

Should I leave her?

Would it save her?

————

Sometimes I think back on the day she noticed she was changing. Sonora had decided to make dinner early. After ten minutes I'd heard a crash and tinkle from the kitchen.

"Goddammit! What the hell?!"

"What happened?" I braced myself against the kitchen doorway, blocking Charlie's inquisitive nose from the glittery crimson carnage of a jar of tomato sauce.

"I was holding it! It jumped out of my hands!" She stared at her palms, a combined awe and rage suffusing her face. Her fingers were shaking, reddened at the tips.

"Cmere." I reached my hand out. "Hop over the glass. I'll clean this mess while you wash your feet."

She grabbed my fingers and jumped. My stomach fell away at her landing, her tilt and sway as she tried to recover her balance. When had her legs gotten so thin?

She turned to glare at the glass shards, then glanced at me, frustration like pickled grapefruit rind rising from her skin.

"What's wrong with me, Kari?"

"Nothing's wrong with you, 'Nora." I squeezed her hand. "I'll take care of this."

"Thanks, hon." She lifted her chin to kiss me. I turned away.

"Take Charlie with you to the bathroom, 'k?"

"Kari?" She grabbed my arm, searching my face. "What's wrong?"

I patted her hand and smiled, my muscles whining with the effort. "Nothing's wrong, baby. I want to get rid of this glass before Charlie sniffs around. Go wash."

She nodded and turned away. She could tell I was lying.

We fought about it later. She came for a kiss before her evening bath, and I turned from her again.

"Okay, what the actual fuck, Kari?"

"What?" I cringed at the stench of my guilt.

"Why don't you want to kiss me?"

She ripped apart excuse after excuse until I came up with the right words, around tears. "I think I'm making you sick, baby. I don't want to make you worse."

She'd burst out laughing, obviously relieved. "Jesus, Kari, you scared the shit out of me. You're not making me sick. You don't have *that* much power." She shoved me lightly.

"Now kiss me, you jerk, before I decide you don't love me anymore."

I could almost feel the grind, her words kneading the hard chunks of my broken heart, as I held her face in my hands. I steeled myself and kissed her, keeping my eyes open for the first time in my life. Our mouths met, the bitterness and sweetness commingling, and I watched as ghostly iridescent filaments coalesced on her skin, swirling down to where our mouths joined.

I almost threw up.

I clenched my eyes closed and finished the kiss, then stood up. "I'm sorry I freaked you out, baby. Go have your bath. I'll walk Charlie tonight."

I sobbed the entire walk. When I got home, I blamed my red eyes on a passing car kicking crap into my eyes.

I'm sure she knew I was lying then, too.

————

"Kari?"

"How are you doing?" I stroked her cheek, trying to push my own emotions through my fingertips into her skin, even though I knew better. I'd tried before. I've tried asking how at all the places I've gone to for help: all the psychics, the witches, the doctors, the osteopaths. They just looked at me like I was mocking them. Sonora's the only one who knows I mean it. Even though she doesn't believe it.

"God, whatever this is, it freaking hurts." She laughed, a metallic waft of pain on the air. "Maybe I should have stayed asleep."

"You can go back to sleep if you want."

"And miss all this?"

"Miss all what?"

She glared at me.

"This. You. Kari, you know I love you, right?"

"Yeah, and sometimes I wonder why. You might be a little insane."

"Ableist jerk." She rolled her eyes. "You're interesting and sweet and you listen to me and you know what I'm feeling before I do and you really, *really* try to be a good person. Why the hell wouldn't I love you?"

I paused, throat tight, and squeezed her hand. "You know me, baby. I always thought you were an anomaly."

That mischievous twist of lip, again. How did she do that, being in so much pain? "Ohh damn right I am. But you're still a loveable bitch."

That got an honest smile from me. "Fine. I'll be your loveable bitch if you'll be my sexy anomaly."

"Sexy, like this?"

I pressed her hand to my cheek. "Sexy forever."

She sighed dreamily, maple contentment on her breath. "I'll take it."

————

"Are you ready?"

It was our third date. Her grin was the blue-grape fragrance of fresh-bloomed irises as she tugged my hand. I'd never sung in public before, but she loved karaoke, so I went. The first song she chose was 'Hey Mickey'.

"Just sing the chorus with me," she wheedled.

Karaoke was a fireworks display of laughter and groaning and bouncing energy. I sang the whole thing through with her, my voice cracking from disuse. The audience laughed with me as I laughed with myself, and her, and the world.

Karaoke with Sonora tasted like rich vanilla birthday cake, including the candle wax, and I was so happy that I'd found it. That I'd found her.

I wish I'd thought more about it, rather than taking it for granted like a drugstore truffle.

It's the work we put in that makes love what it is. I know that now. The hours of pressure, of struggle. Things which don't make sense when you say them to other people, but which make all the difference in the world to us. Who would understand an argument about kisses?

Who else would understand the desperation as I held her narrow, chilly hand for hours to warm it as the IV dripped its coldness into her? Or the frustration as I tried to give back whatever she shared with me, push the theobromine bitterness of my love back into her skin, as her body tried to repair?

————

Sonora shifted in the bed. I could almost see her bones through her skin, and the air was copper-scented. "Yeah, it's a little intense. I think I need to rest." She sighed, a fleeting wince breaking her façade as she lifted her face to me.

I ignored the sting in my eyes and throat as our lips met because she still, in this much pain, wanted to kiss me.

"You sleep, baby. I'll leave in a bit to walk Charlie."

As she settled back and closed her eyes, the nurse glanced at me, sympathy obvious on his face. At this point I'd seen, and smelled, enough of the nurses to know what that meant. My heart thumped loudly, a knuckle on wood, almost audible through my chest. I stroked Sonora's hand as the nurse edged closer.

"I'm sorry, for what it's worth," he whispered.

Sorrow was a salt lick, but around his saltiness I smelled something warm, something nourishing. I looked up at him, focusing on his dark blue eyes, as he reached out to touch my shoulder. His scent was intoxicating, like the best mother's kitchen in the world. Like chicken soup and cinnamon.

Oh gods he's attracted to me.

I didn't think. I grabbed his hand from my shoulder and kissed his knuckles long and deep, kept my eyes open and watched those lovely filaments of emotion thrill into my mouth, and I somehow, despite it hurting like bloody breathless hell, pushed them away from my throat into my shoulder and down, down into the hand that was still holding on to Sonora.

He jumped a little but didn't move his hand until I finished. I looked up at him with teary eyes. "Thank you," I whispered, squeezing his fingers before letting go.

"Any time," he murmured as he stepped away.

As I turned back to Sonora, I could see the filaments still soaking into her skin. Holy gods. It made so much sense. My own emotions weren't enough. I didn't generate enough emotion to replace what I took, but I could route others through me. My mouth tasted like a post-drinking binge, sticky-sour and bile-laden, but it was worth it to see her body drinking in those filaments like a thirsty plant drinks water.

Sonora stirred, shifting on the bed, and opened her eyes.

"What did you do? That felt nice." She shifted again, stretching her legs, her ankle bones cracking for the first time in weeks.

I stifled a sob. Love is bitter. But every day we take the bitterness for what it is, grind through it all and come back to each other. I am who I am, and she loves me, and I'm going to make damn sure that our love doesn't kill her. No matter what it does to others.

"What kind of nice? Drugs nice?"

"Seriously, Kari, what was it? My pain is a lot better."

I raised an eyebrow, mimicking her. "If you must know, I bribed the nurse with a kiss to get you better treatment. That's how much I love you."

She cracked a grin. "Jerk. Fine. Don't tell me, then. But if you kissed someone else, you better pay the kiss tax or you're in trouble."

I smiled, smelling the honey-sweetness of delight, and leaned in. Her lips against mine were the purest, richest, most delicious chocolate I have ever tasted.

Fantasy - 2894 words

About the Author

Risa Wolf is a nonbinary pet parent, writer, and collector of fountain pen inks e.g. professional finger-stainer. They build houses for book-ghosts for a living. Their writing can be found in *Apex* and in the Air and Nothingness Press anthology *Upon A Thrice Time.* Risa plays online on Twitter at **@risawolf** and blogs at https://killerpuppytails.com/.

Donors

A huge thanks to all our supporters on Patreon. Join them:
https://www.patreon.com/cossmass

Liz Wells

Anonymous

Aaron Sisto

Orla Hayes

Jessica Hyslop

Chirag Desai

Carol Scheina

Myra Campbell

Elizabeth Campbell

Deanne Fountaine

Jeffery Reynolds

Pauline Barmby

Andrew Leon Hudson

Danielle Mayabb

Devi Lacroix

Evan Dicken

Frances KR

Jean Ward

Kristen Koopman

Rebecca Treasure Schibler

Owen McManus

Lyndsey Croal

Thomas Ha

Support Us

We hope you enjoyed reading *Cossmass Infinities*. Please consider supporting us:

Become a Patron

https://www.patreon.com/cossmass

Newsletter

https://www.cossmass.com/newsletter/

www.ingramcontent.com/pod-product-compliance
Lightning Source LLC
Chambersburg PA
CBHW061513120726
48001CB00004B/1308